Servicing the Work Men
Novellas 1-5

Ruan Willow
Aka Ruin Willow

Table of Contents

Dedication

This book is dedicated to lovers who play in and out of the bedroom, those who never stop playing, and those who desire to please their partners and get off on getting their partner off, plus celebrate who they truly are because that's how it should be. Mutual pleasure is mutual bliss.

This book is an erotic romance, please read and enjoy it knowing this is the genre it is in.

Marinate in your sexuality daily.

Servicing the Trash Man, Her Filthy Hotwife Adventure,

Book 1

Chapter 1

Laney adjusted her sundress for maximum cleavage, which was quite easy, being blessed with double D's. His truck would be rumbling down the street imminently, and she was ready. She paced in front of the tall windows flanking the door. She eagerly peered into the dim early morning sunshine, her heart racing.

John's hands smoothed down her ass cheeks and he cupped each of them in his strong hands. He gave her buns a strong squeeze before leaning in to whisper in her ear, "You ready?" His voice was seductive and commanding, which gave her a delicious clit twitch, which it always did before the dates.

"Yes, John. I'm very ready." She shifted her hips to savor his tightening grabs.

"You fuck him good, alright? I'll be watching." His voice was breathy and full of lusty anticipation, she loved that he seemed ever horny for the benefits of her union too.

The most exciting part was that she never knew when he'd watch the sexual escapades or how he would. He was often out of sight but always watching, which really turned her on. It hit her exhibitionistic streak straight on. That was part of the fun, the not knowing how he'd spy on her with the other man, or when he'd make his appearance. John often arranged the hotwife dates for Laney, but he really loved it when she pursued and set them up herself too. She'd been courting Jaxon, their regular garbage man, to fuck for quite some time. She was ready to go in for the official fuck today. She knew she'd kill it. There was no way he'd say 'no'.

John pressed his erection to her backside and snaked his hands up her front. "Good, no bra. Good girl." He thrust his hardon between her buns and growled. "Can't wait to watch you seduce him. Then I'm reclaiming you. I'm feeling very horny and aggressive already, so you'd better be ready for me."

His words sent shivers through her core and a jolt through her pelvic region.

They'd stepped into the hotwife lifestyle ten months ago and fallen into a fabulous routine. Once a man was chosen, and upon John's approval, they'd fuck. Then John would reclaim her as his woman. Not that he ever gave her away, it was more of a wife share than a giving away of anything. The reclaiming was a delicious fuck loan that needed to be repaid by Laney. She'd happily and lustily submit to his will afterwards. She got to fuck other men and John wanted her to. It gave him an even bigger reason to dominate her, which they both loved.

Their marriage had changed once Laney lost her job. She wasn't able to find another one she liked fast enough and stopped looking once both she and John realized how happy they both were with her being a housewife. She'd worked diligently outside the home all her life, an independent strong woman of forty-three. Well, that hadn't changed, but what did change was that now she took care of their home full time, made gourmet meals, and fucked men on the regular. John never considered her lesser for not pulling in money. They were equal partners, it was just that she didn't get money in exchange for what she did anymore. What she got was happiness, fulfillment, and John got the same. He felt cared for, attended to, and aroused in a way that perfectly met his satiation.

It satisfied her far more than she had ever expected, and she'd drip pussy juice when they'd talk about their plans. The debriefing after the fuck was even yummier.

Laney was astonished. She'd have never thought this would be how she'd be in midlife. She figured she'd be the nurse manager in the hospital or a bigger wig in a company or something, not someone who stayed home all the time. But, in staying home, she'd learned to cook like a gourmet chef, worked out like a gym rat, and made love to her husband every day. Life couldn't be any better.

But then it got better. Way better.

When they started the hotwife way of life, it became off-the-charts spectacular. Like it blew her mind like no other experience ever before in her life. And she was going to get to fuck a new man again.

"I wonder if he will do it?" She glanced back at John as she bit her lip. Her gaze was saucy and sassy.

"I have faith in you. That's the challenge when you find the man," he reminded.

He was right there. When she found the man to have sex with, it was her job to seduce him. Sometimes she had to let the man think she was cheating, at first, but other times she let them in on the secret. Reading the man's turn-ons in the moment always guided her plan. It was like a dance, and she loved the improvisation of the whole flirtation. If she got the man to fuck her, which usually was pretty easy, her reward was John pleasuring her to orgasmic heights after. Then she happily submitted to whatever his sexual whims were at that moment, which varied between punishments to rewards. But either way, they both came hard as cannon blasts.

It had inflamed their sex life to unimaginable highs. It gave a new meaning to the phrase 'getting lucky'.

"Go be your sexy self," John whispered in her ear, his voice full of lust and hunger. "I know you will." He growled like a wolf as he grazed her skin with his beard scruff, and she shuddered.

He gave her one light spank on her right ass cheek as the garbage truck rumbled down the street.

"Go play, babe," he commanded. "Fuck that cock hard."

Her heart did a giddy leap inside her chest and set itself on a rampant pounding. It wouldn't slow down for quite some time, she figured.

Jaxon was a sexy man, and his gaze always gave her butterflies. She couldn't wait for him to swoop out of the truck and approach her, his eyes full of licentious hope.

She pulled the front door open and bounded out into the birthing sunshine. The aroma of flowers blooming flooded her nostrils as the burst of colors delighted her.

Jaxon was late today, which had her hunger for him raging even more.

Barefoot, she sauntered across the grass. She planted herself in her flower garden and waved at him even though he was too far away. She bent over and fixed a flower that didn't really need fixing. She grinned. A girl had to use whatever props were in front of her to draw her prey in.

Jaxon visited all the houses in order as she primped and prodded her already-weeded flower bed. She glanced at the house but couldn't see John in any of the windows. It set her heart beating faster, not knowing where he'd be. Wondering if he was watching her reel in her fucking victim was always thrilling. It was part of the game and John always loved it when she guessed it right from the moment he started watching. At times, John had made it obvious, and at others, he'd stayed hidden until the man left. Thinking of him stroking his cock while he watched her get railed was always so damn hot. It made her come so hard.

Jaxon pulled his truck up to the driveway and she bent over again so he could likely see her bare nipples through the low neckline of her orange sundress.

His eyes lit with desire as he rounded the front end of his garbage truck.

"Hi, Laney," he said breathlessly.

He was panting already. Perfect.

"Hi, Jaxon. Nice morning, isn't it?" She dipped her body forward further so he could get an even better look at her bare tits inside the bodice of her dress.

His smile deepened. "Very nice indeed. I love your flower garden. You weed it so well," he said suggestively as she dug around.

She saw proof that he'd likely to be her willing victim when she spied his erection pressing a bulge out of his pants. She swiveled her ass towards him and doubled over at the waist. The breeze lifted the hem of her sundress slightly and tickled her bare pussy lips. She hoped he was getting a peak. She sighed and said, "Yeah, it's hard work keeping all the weeds at bay all the time. Weeding never ends."

He let out a groan, but didn't acknowledge it as he suggestively said, "You keep it in perfect form."

She grinned. He wasn't talking about her garden at all. "I work at it every day."

"I can tell," he said with a whistle.

She straightened up her spine and slowly swayed her hips exaggeratedly as she walked towards him. She gave him major fuck me eyes before asking, "Have a busy day today? Or it is a low pickup day?"

"Oh, it's not bad. I have a few hours more at the least. But stopping at your house always makes my day. If you ever need an extra pickup, text me." He heckled at his own desperate-sounding voice. "Please?"

She nodded as she grabbed his arm and gazed up into his soft brown eyes. They were brimming with desire. "Sure thing," she said with assurance as she pressed her bosom to him.

He drew in a deep breath and looked very happy that she was touching him, which made her very happy.

"I appreciate that, Jaxon. You're a gem for offering. I may ask you for something extra with your service."

"It gets to be a lonely job, not much interaction with others. So, I always enjoy our chats." His face softened as he held her gaze.

"I do too." She released his arm, but then captured it again in an embrace of her breasts. "Very much so. You are so kind to talk with me."

He grinned salaciously as she shimmied her breasts against his arm. "You have such nice …"

She smiled devilishly as he struggled for his next words. "Boobies?" she asked, to help him out.

He laughed heartily, his belly bouncing in tune. "Yes."

"And … other parts," she said suggestively.

"Yes," he said with less unease. "I'm glad you said it and not me." He glanced around at the neighbor's homes. "Your husband home today?"

"Oh, yes, he is." She didn't plan on hiding anything from Jaxon. He'd flirted with her so many times when John was home that she had concluded that he wasn't going to mind the whole hotwife thing. It was a risk, of course, to consider telling him; she might lose the fuck, and get a freakish look, but she had a sneaking suspicion that Jaxon would be into it. And honestly, she didn't care if he wasn't. His loss. She'd just move on to the next cock.

"I see. He must keep pretty busy working from home most days?" Jaxon was fishing for info, and it was part of the fun of the game.

She gave him a frisky twinkling look. "Yes, he has many meetings he has to be on for hours most days. But not today. He has no meetings right now." A surge of empowerment rippled across her chest, which was a badge of confidence she'd earned since hotwifing. She stepped in front of Jaxon and bent over to pick a weed in the grass. She backed up a step, then another, so her ass pressed smack against his hardon.

"Wow," he muttered in awe. "I didn't expect."

She giggled with innocence, which made her butt cheeks move against his engorged penis.

"Oh, my God," he muttered. He drew in a deep gasp.

"Oh, sorry about that, I just saw another weed, so I snatched it up. My bad." She stood up and faced him, her cheeks flushed in excitement. Coming on to him this aggressively was embarrassing, but that was a turn on in and of itself. She wanted him to think she was desperate, so she boldly moved to him and pressed her tits against his canvas work shirt. "I don't suppose you'd be able to help me move a piece of garbage from the garage, would you?"

"Oh, I'd be happy to help you." His expression was dopey, but he looked so happy.

She wondered if he thought she was just going to flash him, or if he knew her come-ons meant something more. She hoped he wanted more. She peered around for John but saw no sign of him. She grabbed Jaxon's arm again and smashed her breasts against his thick arm. "I need a strong man like you to do what I need." If he didn't have an inkling that she was seducing him, this man would have to have been a dunce. And if he was that stupid, he didn't deserve her pussy.

She dragged Jaxon along towards the garage, glancing around to see if any neighbors were watching, and she had high hopes at least one was catching this whole scene. Her neighbor to the right had watched her and Jaxon flirt many times, then he'd come out to get a closer look while pretending to do yard work. She had asked John to approach him about fucking her too, but John said he had his reasons why he wasn't going to do that. At least, not yet. It just made her all the more intrigued.

Her pussy lips were wet and slid against each other as she tugged Jaxon into the garage. Near her husband's workbench, they'd added a sex chair and a couch they wouldn't mind getting cum on. No one but them ever came into their garage anyway, so they'd had zero questionable glances about the additions.

Jaxon stopped cold and stared at the sex furniture. "Is that what I think it is?" He was aghast, but clearly pleased.

"Yes." She pulled him over to the blow-up couch with the loops for cuffs on the sides and flung herself over it. She loved being this desperate, it was a bit humiliating, which made her want thicken even more for Jaxon's cock. She yearned to just bare her bottom and raise it up, presenting her holes to him. She pressed the blown up fuck toy all over. "I think this might have a hole in it and we might need to throw it away. Will you check it for me?"

"Gladly," he said. He lined up next to her and began to fondle the couch with his calloused hands. His rough grabs of the plastic made her want his hands on her bare skin even more. "I don't feel anything." He leaned down and placed his ear near it. "I don't hear any hissing sounds of air escaping either."

"Oh," she said innocently. "Okay. Maybe it needs some pressure applied before we can really know."

He chuckled exuberantly. "You going to jump on it?" He looked as if he wished this would happen.

"Good idea," she said exuberantly. She climbed up on top and began to jump. Her bra-less tits flopped heavily with each landing and her sundress flew up, giving him peeks at her bare pussy. She heard a snicker from the back corner of the garage. She sharply glanced over and saw John's shoulder silhouetted. He was pretty camouflaged, so she didn't think Jaxon would notice.

Jaxon pressed himself down harder and listened. To her delight, he seemed to be looking up her skirt at the same time as he dragged his ear around the surface of the blown-up couch. "I don't hear a thing. I think it might be okay. Would be a shame if it had a hole. You'd need to patch it." His smile was so big she thought it might break his face in half.

Instantly, she was overwhelmed with the urge to indulge his cock and let him slide it up her cunt. She stopped jumping and sat down, pressing her bare pussy to the plastic, and smearing her juices across it as she slid off. "It might need something stronger to test it, I'm thinking."

Jaxon cocked his head to the side. "I could punch it?"

She smiled and gave him a demure look. This was the point at which she and John called the 'hook and reel in'. She relinquished any pesky reservations and stated, "Or you could fuck me over it. That might likely do it."

He took a step back, his face frozen in an expression of utter shock.

She didn't move, but kept the devilish look on her face.

He stammered, "Are you being serious? Because if you are ..."

"Oh, I'm very serious, Jaxon. Will you fuck me?" She smiled at him and pursed her lips. "Please?" she begged as her breathing began to ramp up.

He blinked several times before stroking his goatee. His dick looked even bigger beneath his work pants. "Your husband around, though?"

She loved that he seemed tempted without knowing more and gave him a very pleased expression. "He is around. But Jaxon, I'm a hotwife."

His smirk grew into a lecherous, yet appreciative look. "Oh, yeah? Is that so?" He looked as if he knew he was about to get lucky, and it made Laney want to submit to his will even more.

"Yes, and he wants other men to fuck me. He gets off on it." She was ecstatic he knew what a hotwife was.

His eyes widened, but the smile never left his lips as he asked, "A cuck? No shit?"

She shook her head as she took a step towards him. "Not exactly. No. He sets up sex dates for me. Then watches me get fucked, then he fucks me himself." She grinned lasciviously.

His eyes turned skeptical. "Does he know you are doing this right now, by chance?" His tone was almost hopeful.

"Yes. He told me to seduce you. You see, John is a dominant who likes to share me." She pressed her forefinger into her mouth and sucked it. "But he knew I wanted to fuck you, because I told him. He's watched almost all of our flirtations from inside the house."

He dropped his jaw, but his eyes lit with joy. "For real?"

"Yes. Are you in?" Her heart did a pitter-patter as she approached the kill. She didn't want John's help, she was determined to snag him herself.

"Well, I guess I am if your husband is on board." He glanced back at his truck as it rumbled a bit louder while idling. "Wouldn't take long, I suppose."

She snickered. "No. Not likely. I'm pretty hot, and I'm guessing you are the same."

He rubbed his hands together. "Damn straight I am. You're sexy as fuck. I never expected this today. Or ever." He glanced around the garage. "He in here somewhere hiding?"

"Yes," she admitted. "But I don't know where he is."

"Smart man," Jaxon said, not looking a bit scared. "I wouldn't mind watching his reclaiming of you, if it turned you guys on." He seemed full of anticipation that she'd say yes.

"We can ask him. After. It would certainly turn me on." She strode up to him and stroked his face. "What do you say? You wanna fuck?"

His face blossomed into someone who had just won the lottery. "Damn right I do, darling."

She pressed her body to his, loving the feeling of this taboo act in her own garage, and with her husband watching. She imagined John had his own hard dick out and was stroking it.

He bent down to kiss her. He tasted like coffee and donuts as she savored his tongue against hers. She was very thankful that he didn't smell like trash. His hands cupped her ass and he groaned.

"Wow," he muttered as lust blazed in his eyes.

She moaned in response, ecstatic to finally have his hands on her.

"Fuck, I haven't had sex in a few years," he slurred as he suckled her neck.

"High time then," she whispered into his mouth before they kissed again. The mound at his crotch felt like a brick against her abdomen. "You seem quite ready to shove that inside me."

"Oh, you have no idea," he said, so full of desire it made her clit twitch.

He might not think so, but she fully got it. She'd found she had a particular affinity for satiating men who hadn't had sex in a long time. Their passion was always bright as the sun, short-lived as it was. They often came quickly, but it was always hot and brilliant while it lasted, like the explosion of fireworks. She knew if she didn't come, it never mattered. John would make her come multiple times when it came his turn at her used wet pussy. But she'd delightfully realized that most men wanted to make her come. She'd had a few narcissistic men in her time who hadn't cared, but being used was also a kink of hers. And again, she had John, who always made sure he was sexually satisfied and fully spent before the day was done. He was her king, and she was his queen. And as much as she wanted him sexually satiated, he wanted it more for her.

Jaxon's hands traveled her body, shifting her sundress, revealing her flesh to expose various parts of her. He always had an air of hunger about him when they'd flirted, maybe it was because she'd engaged him. She'd blatantly sought out his attention by flirting with him every Friday.

"Fuck, you are so fucking hot," he blurted in a strained voice.

Her only hope was he wouldn't come in his pants before he shoved himself inside her wet, slutty hole. She needed to move this along. "How do you want me, Jaxon?" she writhed seductively against his torso. "I'm really horny and I want your cock inside me."

He guffawed. "This is like my fantasy coming true. Fuck." He cleared his throat and looked around. "I won't lie, I've fantasized about fucking you. But are you sure your husband isn't going to appear out of a dark shadow with a raised hammer for my head?" He seemed to be joking, but a bit serious.

"It's all good," John called loudly. "Fuck her. Then you can watch me fuck her." It was a command, not a suggestion. "She gets off on dirty talk." It was a shorter briefing than his usual, but it made her feel special nonetheless.

She grinned in a gloat, super happy John revealed himself, and he was on board with letting Jaxon watch him take her. She was thrilled! This was a gift!

"Oh, well, I'll be damned, I've fallen into a real-life porno." He laughed with glee. "How did I get this lucky today?"

She twirled in front of him, so her sundress flared, then she bent over to show him her tits once more. "Because I wanted you. Now. Take me, I'm yours, Jaxon." Well, really, he was hers, but she wasn't about to point that fact out.

He opened his arms and she rushed into them.

"Yes, I want this. How will you fuck me?" she pressed him again.

"If you're my slut for the moment, I definitely want you doggy. But I'd like to see my whoring slut naked first."

She took a step back and lifted her arms over her head. "Do the honors," she instructed. She was acutely aware that the garage door was wide open and any one of the neighbors could catch a glimpse of her naked booty. But this made it all the more exhilarating.

He lunged at her and flung her sundress off so quickly she gasped.

"Wow, fuck, you are unbelievable," he seethed through clenched teeth. "Perfect."

"Oh, you've seen them. I've all but flashed you at least twenty times," she snickered.

"It's not the same as seeing you fully bare naked. You're stunning. Gorgeous."

She beamed at his sexy compliment and spun for him when he motioned his forefinger in a circle.

"Your husband is a very lucky man indeed." He whistled. "Shit. No shit."

"Yes, I am," John answered, which was a scrumptious reminder that her loving husband was still watching.

Jaxon grabbed her and turned her around faster than she could think it. He bent her over and caressed her bare bottom in one fell swoop of his hand. His hunger for her was evident, and it wet her pussy more.

She moaned out her appreciation of his gruff touching as he next meandered his hands to cup her hanging breasts.

"Oh, fuck me," he muttered. "I can't believe I get to do this to you."

His breath along the flesh of her back was seductive, and her pussy lips flared slightly open. He pressed his fingers along her slit with his other hand and she knew she was in for a climax with how he worked her pussy into a lather.

"You like it like this?" he asked as he rubbed her clit aggressively.

"Yes," she moaned. "And more. Harder. I like it hard." She barely got the words out. She was already panting so fast.

"I get off on you coming first, so tell me how you like it." His declaration yanked her climax to the edge.

"Mmmm," she moaned. "Yeah, that. More of that." She rocked her hips, trying to get as much of his finger pressing along her slit and lips as she could. When he molested her clitoral head in rough rubs, she cried out, "Yes, oh my fuck me, yes!" She gasped as her moans increased in intensity. "Just like that." She clutched at the couch, but it was too full of air to get a handful, so she curled her fingers to her palms instead. Within thirty seconds, he had her ready to climax.

She loved that she was naked, and he was still clothed as he was well on his way to making her come. But she also couldn't wait to see his cock.

"Gonna come," she said between big whimpers. "Please, don't stop, Jaxon."

He didn't respond, but roughed up her clit even more vigorously. With his hot breath on her back and his fat erection pressed to her, she came hard. She released a cry before her body began its orgasm curl. Her eyes rolled and her eyelids fluttered as she gasped out her peak. Her body twitched as she finished the orgasm.

"Oh, fuck, that was so good," she said in a soft gratified voice. "So good, Jaxon. So good."

He slowed his finger movements but kept himself pressed to her backside.

"Now beat up my pussy with that cock," she pleaded.

He laughed with abandon. "That won't be a tough task at all, darling." She heard the sound of his metal zipper being unzipped and it sent a zing of excited energy through her, which amplified when he presented his packed cock head at her opening.

She tried to get a glimpse of his cock, but he was too eager.

He roughly entered her hole, but he slid right in with ease because of her juices. He began pounding her from behind like a beast in heat. His grunts drove up her passion to an unbridled level as he smacked into her butt from behind. Her tits were swinging violently as John appeared out of the shadows.

She smiled as Jaxon rocked her body. This was a delicious part.

His grin was big and carnal as he watched Jaxon fuck her primal like a wild bear. Within a minute, Jaxon gave a deep growl, then railed her with deep strokes, shaking her body violently against his relentless thrusts.

She cried out and hollered as he hungrily used her slippery hole right in front of her husband's approving gaze.

It was so hot she was ready to burst into flames.

"Fuck her good and hard, Jaxon. Get her ready for me." John looked smug and she loved pleasing him this way. Jaxon was doing John a favor because she was getting hungrier for John's cock by the second.

Jaxon grunted as he ravished her.

"Good slut," John stated as he stared intently into her eyes.

She played with her clit as Jaxon took his pleasure from her pussy. She came again, this time with a smaller orgasm, but still one, and that's all that mattered. Her walls clenched around his cock inside her womb, and he groaned deeply.

He pulled his cock out and his hot cum splattered across her skin.

She savored the wet sounds as he stroked his wet cock milking it all out to coat her.

"Oh, fuck," he said, sounding satisfied. "That was the best fuck ever."

"Rub your cum into my skin, Jaxon," she pleaded.

He snorted, but obeyed. "Never had a woman like you before. That was incredible."

His hands spread his cum across her lower back and buttocks. She smirked as he ran his hands along her hips too. As his cum dried on her, John uncrossed his arms.

"Thank you," Jaxon stated meekly. "Never in my life have I ever." He took a few steps back from her backside and said, "Whew! Holy fuck."

"Thank you," said John sternly. "I thank every man who makes my beautiful wife come. She deserves to come as many times as she desires."

"Aw, I got you now," Jaxon stated. "I get it. You really are a smart man."

"Yes, and now I get whatever I want from her. And she loves giving it to me." John's voice was very matter of fact as he securely locked her hips between his hands. He pressed his hardon to the crevice between her cheeks. "You can go over there where I had been standing."

John stepped away from her and she shuddered because she guessed this time he'd wanted to punish her a bit.

His hand smacked her ass hard three times. "You naughty little whore."

She winced from each whack, but the reverberations through her aroused clit rang up her next climax nicely. It wouldn't take her much to climax again. She met Jaxon's eyes as John spanked her once more.

He laughed and nodded. "Nice," he said appreciatively. He was clearly enjoying the punishment almost as much as the two of them were, maybe more.

The humiliation of being spanked in front of another man, especially one who had just had his cock inside her, was titillating. Not gonna lie. She whimpered and moaned as John hit her right ass cheek with his hard cock. This was something to talk about more after.

He fondled her hanging nips and yanked on them repeatedly.

She yelped and Jaxon nodded again. "That's right," he said with a filthy smirk.

John slapped her ass once more. "Who's your king?" he commanded.

"You are, Sir." Her voice was barely audible.

"That's right. You're mine and mine alone." He caressed her bottom before visiting her lower lips with the tips of his fingers. "Mmmm, nice and wet. Good work, Jaxon."

She found it interesting he kept acknowledging Jaxon. Her husband was so wonderful, she never knew what he'd do next, and the surprises always added more spice to whatever they were doing. The novelty made the whole scene even more titillating when he'd do something new like this.

"Fuck me, I'm yours, Sir." Sometimes he was 'Daddy', sometimes he was 'Sir', but regardless, she submitted happily to his will every damn time, which still astonished her.

John pressed his cockhead inside her. "Mine. You're mine. All mine."

"Yes," she said, shaking her head against the plastic. Her body bounced on the blow-up couch as he fucked her increasingly harder by the second. She watched Jaxon's face as her husband fucked her roughly doggy style and it flared her passion higher. "More." When John pressed her clit, she screamed out, "I'm gonna—"

He left her clit and selfishly rammed himself to the hilt inside her, successfully arousing her G-spot to the max point. She scrambled to catch her chance at another orgasm and spanked her external clit head, then rubbed it. She came first, then John grunted several times before pumping himself into her even harder and faster. He spewed his cum up inside her contracting vagina.

"Oh, fuck," she gasped out. "That was big big big."

He slowed his thrusting, but remained inside. He rubbed her back and sides. "Good girl, very good girl."

She collapsed on the couch, now cum drunk with a floaty-soaring feeling. "Holy fucking shit," she managed to say as both men stared down at her with giant grins.

"You can say that again," John said through his panting.

Seeing both men looking pleased added to her enjoyment of it all. "Best threesome yet," she cooed.

John nodded. "Yeah, for me too. That was totally unexpected. I didn't plan to reveal myself. Was just gonna fuck you after he left, but changed my mind."

Jaxon scoffed. "Well, I'm glad you did. I was half expecting you to come running at me like a madman and beat the shit out of me."

"Nope. That's not how we roll." John extended his hand to Jaxon, and they shook hands over Laney's naked body.

With both men still dressed, and only John's cock out, it felt even more taboo to be spread out fully nude beneath them. But, honestly, she felt worshipped like a queen under their handshake. She was the sex goddess they had served. She'd come the most of the three of them and gotten the most pleasure. But then, that was her goal from the start.

Jaxon shrugged. "Well, thanks for the fuck. I'd better get back to it. I'm a bit off schedule now."

She giggled. "I've been enjoying wondering if the neighbors have wondered what's going on with your truck just parked at our house and still running this whole time."

He chuckled. "Well, if they see my grin, they might know something."

"Thanks, Jaxon, for playing along with my wife's wishes."

"Oh, it was my pleasure. Anytime. Count me in." He waved and walked down the driveway.

John scooped her up and they watched Jaxon move on to the neighbor's garbage can.

She gazed into John's eyes. "I just fucked our garbage man. And I feel incredible."

"As you should, babe. Now let's head inside and have some breakfast. I want to satiate you another way."

"I love you, John." She smiled. "Look at you, with that satisfied grin, my wonderful husband."

He winked back. "I love you all through eternity."

She soaked up the sappy affirmations of love and prepared her tummy with the thoughts of an omelet and coffee. She laughed as he carried her up the stairs to the door. "He tasted like coffee. I didn't think my first taste of coffee of the day would come from our garbage man's mouth."

John laughed heartily as he carried her across the threshold. "Now that's a one-liner you don't hear often."

"Like never!"

He set her down and she went to grab her robe as he headed for the kitchen. The day was off to the best start she could ever want, and it was only 8:00 in the morning.

Servicing the Pool Man, Her Filthy Hotwife Adventure

Book 2

Chapter 1

Laney rolled to her side and glanced at her phone. Lounging by the pool in the brilliant afternoon sun felt so yummy after a very physical morning of cooking, a vigorous round of sex with John, and then working out for an hour. Being a housewife was much more physical than she'd imagined it would be, at least for a hard-working nympho gym rat like her. But she was most definitely a wanton slut, that was topmost. She was already full of desire to come again, but she knew John was in an important meeting.

Overcome with horniness, she slipped her hand inside her suit bottoms and played with her pussy lips. John had made her climax nine times this morning already but come afternoon time and she was yearning to peak again. She was indeed relentless with her libido, and she loved it. She'd always had a rise in her desire in the afternoons, and she loved succumbing to it. But the thought John loved it even more. But, she sighed, he was deep in work planning and not available for any pleasuring now. She grinned with relish. But that didn't mean she couldn't indulge.

She'd already prepped dinner, so lounging by the pool seemed like the best idea ever, and masturbating poolside in the blazing sun was an even better idea. So why the fuck not?

She glanced at the house and knew it was possible John might look out the window from his desk and see her touching herself during his afternoon meeting. She hoped he did. He loved her playing the exhibitionist. She had half a mind to text him and tell him to look out and watch. He'd come out and fuck her for sure if she did, so she decided to bring herself to climax first on her own. He needed to get work done. He had a big project coming due at work that had been giving him loads of stress. She'd gotten to help with relieving it by giving him head during meetings from beneath his desk. The memories were helping her arousal climb.

She rubbed her lips while they were still closed as she reminisced further, her slit still sealed off like a wrapped gift. She pressed her puffy lips, and a moan escaped her other lips. A primal one, not one of thought or any kind of purpose.

It was just a sound that bubbled from her gut. No sentences were needed. That would get her stuck in her head when she needed to be feeling her body. It was one of the wonderful things she'd learned to do well recently.

She mashed and kneaded her lips, pressing harder on the cleft of her lower lips over her clit. The jewel of her womanhood beneath was scrumptiously waking up and ready for action. Slipping a finger inside her fleshy lips, she felt her wetness overflowing already. She smiled and pushed another finger inside and began to rapidly finger fuck herself. She wasn't nearly as good at it as John, but she could get herself off in time. Her arms were just too short to get the power he could.

She loved this type of thing. Being on display, potentially being watched while being sexual, or even more so, actual blatant watching. It really churned her into a delicious, hot mess. Nakedness in semi-public was a switch that ticked her enjoyment higher, so she always took advantage when she could, even in her own backyard.

She again reflected on how their sex life had changed from one of doldrums to magnificently wow. Before John latched on to her midlife sexual awakening and embarked on his own journey, their relations had been blah and routine, like a series of checkboxes. He hadn't really gotten her off most times, either. It had gotten so bad it was really only one out of ten, and only when they used sex toys. But now both their marriage and sex were beyond glorious, exciting, an ever-evolving state of pure bliss.

She smiled, remembering when that flip of the switch occurred and John realized his inner Dom. She went from avoiding sex to initiating with him, and he went from lazy lover to stag. They'd literally exploded. She half expected their sexual energy to blow the roof off the house most days. The local community of swingers they'd found had been paramount in the fruition of John's transformation, and she'd be forever grateful.

She slipped her swimsuit top off her right breast and caressed her hardening nipple. The raised map of her tit fleshed itself out quickly as she played. With the sun beating down on her bare skin, she soaked up the warmth from the sky and the building heat between her thighs. Thoughts of Jaxon fucking her in the garage the other day ramped up her excitement. Reminiscing then how John took over and fucked her in front of him brought her looming climax closer.

Being a hotwife was turning out to be even more fun than she'd expected. It was a gift John gave her every day. One that she never took for granted because she got to fuck other men and it turned him on to share her, then fuck her himself. If someone had told her a premonition that this all would happen in her midlife, she would have called them crazy, an insane lunatic.

The memories of the other day played in her head like a reel. Her arousal reached a top max as she recalled how Jaxon's face had been so sexy as he had egged her husband on to fuck her. How hot that had been!

"Oh, fuck, yes," she muttered as she undid the straps of her swimsuit so she could shove her bottoms down to her knees. Free from the prison of the suit, she freely spanked her clitoris with her fingers.

This rough move always launched her. She gyrated her hips, unable to keep her body still anymore.

"Ooooh," she gasped, then moaned. The orgasm was coming for her fast. She slowed down her spanking for a moment to savor.

The aroma of ylang ylang wafted off her chest and pleased her. Flaky remnants of dried lube littered her chest where John had titty fucked her after their breakfast of freshly made omelets. She'd cooked naked, with only a cooking apron on. John told her she was lucky he wanted her fully fed before he took her bent over the kitchen table, otherwise the food would have gotten cold while he fucked her. Her satisfaction had become his top priority, which made her want to do anything he desired back. She was indeed a very lucky girl.

All the images and sensations of recent sessions of sex rolled about in her brain, one by one, some with John, some with others. They were feeding her lust as she rubbed her clitoral head hard. She moaned and grunted as she writhed on the mesh of the lounge beach chair. The bubbling of the water in the pool fountain beside her added to her pleasure as she bared her other nipple to molest it.

She groaned out loud enough for people on the path behind their house to hear. She didn't hold back at all and let her natural sounds pierce the air.

The orgasm got its full grip on her. It won like a champ against her attempts to edge longer, sending her into the no-stop zone. Retreat was no longer possible. She came hard, her body curling forward as her legs bent and stiffened. She twitched and sputtered as her strong vaginal walls sent out contraction after contraction.

"Oh, fuck," she blurted involuntarily. "Oh, shit!" she gasped. "Big big big." Like she usually told John, describing what her body was taking her through. He always wanted to know everything she was feeling, and she loved that so very much.

She heard a male gasp.

She froze in place, startled. As she glanced around, she saw nothing until she spied the top of a head over the top edge of the fence. More of the face appeared as whoever it was made eye contact with her. He looked familiar, but she couldn't place him without seeing more.

"I'm sorry." It was Anderson, their pool boy. Though he was more a man than a boy with a body to die for and eyes that were jovial and kind. "Sorry," he shouted again, sounding terrified. "I'm so sorry. I didn't mean to watch, Laney."

Three sorry's. Wow. He must be really freaked out. But she guessed he did just watch her masturbate without her knowing. He had no idea that was something she loved.

Most people might cover up, but she glanced down at her bared tits and uncovered pussy and grinned. Anderson was another of the workmen who came to the house regularly that she wanted to fuck. She'd told John about wanting Anderson, so immediately she wondered if John had already talked with Anderson about fucking her, knowing that he'd just peeping-tomed at her.

"I just heard a sound and so that's why I looked." He was cute trying to justify his voyeurism into something innocent, which she expected it totally wasn't. His cheeks flared a deep red. "I couldn't look away." He looked like a sheepish little child who had stolen a chocolate bar in the store and had already eaten it.

"Oh, hello, Anderson. It's okay." She didn't bother to fix her bathing suit to cover her nakedness because the truth was, she liked him looking at her and it stroked her libido. John was going to get some good head after this.

He smiled and lust filled his eyes. "I didn't expect the sound to be ... that."

She laughed and sat up, still leaving her large breasts bare as they swung with her movements, then settled. "I got a little carried away, I guess. I was seized by a desire to play with myself all of a sudden."

"That's... that's ...just ... just ... hot. Wow!" he said in a stutter, with an amazed look. But his expression turned guilty again and he dipped back below the top of the fence so she couldn't see much of him anymore. "Oh, I shouldn't be looking at you like that. Is your husband home? I had a few questions about what he wanted done to the pool. Unless you know?" he asked hopefully.

She jumped as a loud clunk of something hitting the fence hard rang out across the yard.

"Oh, damn! John! I didn't hear you come up." Anderson sounded so panicked she felt bad for him. "I didn't mean to …"

"Anderson, it's okay. Hey, you want to come in for a beer? It's a hot day and I bet you've been out in the sun boiling all day long and could use a nice cold beer in the air conditioning."

The silence that followed was almost comical. She wished she could see Anderson's face shifting through the myriad of expressions she figured it must be. But she imagined he must look very confused as the topmost one.

"Come," John said invitingly. "Let's share a beer and we can talk about the pool."

Anderson mumbled something inaudible, which made her smile. She loved that he was flustered.

John opened the fence door and smiled at her. "Looking sexy and beautiful, Laney. Looking forward to hearing what that was all about." He twirled his fingers in the air in her direction.

Anderson stopped in his tracks and stared at her mostly naked body, then looked at John, then back to her, then back to John. He looked as bewildered as he possibly could.

"Are you serious, sir?" Anderson asked with a voice full of questioning. "I thought you'd be firing me right about now or punching me in the face."

"Nope. My good young man, why don't you come inside, and we can chat? I definitely am not firing you. In fact, I'd like to talk with you about something else entirely, in addition to the pool."

The giddiness of the potential of Anderson fucking her today filled her entire body with electricity. John gave her a knowing nod as he ushered the handsome Mr. Anderson Faulkner into the basement. He gave her another nod and then both men were out of sight.

That was reassuring, she would kill to be a fly on the wall, but instead, she eyed up the clear inviting pool water before her, fully stripped her suit bottoms off, and dove in.

Gliding in the water nude was perfection as the water caressed her bare nipples, swished along her thighs, seeped between her labia lips to refresh her warm, still swollen slit. It was a slice of heaven, especially after climaxing in the open air and sunshine.

As she made her third lap across the pool, the sliding door opened and her husband, and an astonished, but happy-looking, Anderson emerged.

Her heart fluttered at the looks on their faces. If that was any indication of the future, maybe she'd get to be fucked by Anderson after all.

Chapter 2

"Hi, baby. How's the water?" John asked affectionately. "Skinny dipping, I see."

"Yes. Omigod, it feels so amazing. I love swimming naked. It always feels so incredible to swim, but without anything on, it feels even more incredible."

He knew this, but he also knew she'd said it for Anderson. "You look sexy as fuck, baby." He grinned so big and, by the look in his eyes, his talk with Anderson clearly had gone well. "Go on, Anderson. You can tell her what you think of her body. She loves to hear it. Tell her what you just told me."

Anderson stared at her with wide eyes, then his face melted into an inviting smile. It turned her insides to mush. He was so sweet and cute and sexy all at once. A real strong and rugged-looking man with large biceps and what looked like maybe washboard abs might be beneath his dri-weave shirt because it clung snugly to his tapered torso. She'd longed to see him shirtless again. It had only happened once two summers ago when she'd been home early from work because of a late afternoon dentist appointment. She'd just gone home instead of going back to work after, and there was a feast for her eyes in her own backyard. Anderson was doing an extra job building a retaining wall and he was lugging big cement blocks and stacking them like they were toy blocks. His muscles had shone with sweat in the sunshine, flexing and releasing as he manhandled the heavy blocks with ease. Her pussy had swam in a puddle of her feminine juices as she watched him. She'd gone off and masturbated and not told John a thing. Back then their marriage had been very different.

She swam through the water, getting more aroused by the second. Anderson's eyes revealed a devilish twinkle he'd never shown her before. She liked it. A lot. Her pussy slit flared slightly as she watched his expression grow even more voracious as she emerged from the water, her breasts bobbing.

"Wow," he muttered, aghast, but with appreciation. "You are unbelievably beautiful." His jaw dropped slightly.

"You can say more, Anderson. Remember what I told you." John's voice was fatherly, nurturing.

Anderson cleared his throat. "You are the sexiest woman I've ever had the pleasure to be in the presence of. You are a goddess. And I've always thought so, and now I know so."

She smiled at him and bit her lip flirtatiously. Her eyes drifted down his body and landed on the significant bulge at his crotch. He was clearly sporting a nice erection, and she wanted it.

"Thank you," she said as she stepped onto the concrete. "Oh, it's hot!" She jumped and her breasts and ass cheeks bounced.

"Fuck," Anderson blurted out loudly.

She wondered if it was out of concern for her discomfort or because he loved seeing her lush female curves bounce. She liked both reasons.

John chuckled, then hurried over to grab her flip-flops for her. "Here baby, no need to burn your beautiful feet."

"Thank you, Daddy," she said seductively. She held his gaze as he nodded. Her eyes drifted to Anderson to assess how he took her calling John 'Daddy'.

He looked amused, so she smiled back.

John grabbed her chin with his thumb and forefinger and forced her face his way. Looking her in the eyes, he said, "It's all set, babe. He's going to fuck you, my sweet baby. I'll be watching. Have fun. Then be ready, because I'm going to rail you hard afterwards to claim you back." He took a step away from her, then said in a loud voice. "Go play, babe."

He disappeared into the house as Anderson watched him leave. Anderson stared at the shut door.

She confidently strode closer to him.

He swung his eyes towards her. "Is this for real? Am I dreaming? Like in a coma or something? Or am I dead and in heaven?" His face was not only incredulous, but giddy.

"Oh, no, Anderson. This is very real. I'm sure my husband explained I'm a hotwife, right?" She still longed to know exactly what they talked about, but she knew she'd never get the skinny on that.

"I thought that was a made-up fantasy thing, just in porn, or over in Europe," he said with a light-hearted chuckle.

"Nope, it happens here in the US too. I know many couples who live the hotwife life, or swing. It's more common than you'd think."

"Wow, I'm like frozen I'm so flabbergasted." His eyes were wide but he looked ready to pounce on her.

"I can see that. Well, your cock doesn't seem to be in shock."

He laughed. "Nope. He's quite awake."

"I really want to see your cock. Will you show me?"

He fondled the top of his shorts at the waistband with a lecherous grin. "I can't believe I'm going to get to do this."

"This?" she asked with a snicker. "You mean fuck me?"

He nodded dumbly, but his eyes raged with passion. "Yes."

John opened the door and set her pair of red high heels on the cement step. "He really likes high heels, babe. I knew you'd like to please him." John gave them a salacious smile. She knew he was excited to watch, and that excited her even more.

"Oh, high heels, huh? I'd like to know what else turns you on, Anderson." She desired deeply to satisfy his fantasies.

"You do. You've always turned me on." He stared at her breasts. "That was no lie. I've fantasized about fucking you, if I'm being honest. But never with your husband's permission." He paused and shook his head. "This is just wild."

"I know it is, but it's fantastic, right? We enjoy it so much. I want you to enjoy it too," she cooed.

He belly laughed. "There's zero chance of that not happening."

She couldn't stop imagining him thrusting into her. It was getting so fucking hot to think about. "Good." She sashayed her hips as she walked past him, enjoying every second of his eyes being glued to her. Each moment ticked her raging clit a notch higher.

She slipped off her flip-flops and toed her right foot into the high-heeled shoe, then her left. She glanced backward at him to see if he was watching her ass. She smiled back at him before she swiveled to face him. She couldn't wait for him to fuck her while she had only heels on.

"Boob man? Ass man? Pussy man?" she asked with an arch of her left eyebrow.

He snickered, showing her his horny nature. "Yes!"

"No top fave?" She wanted to know his turn-ons, his hot buttons so she could make him come hard.

"I guess boob man, but I love all parts of a woman's body, honestly. I am infatuated with the female form, like most."

She got the impression he was not like most men at all. She caressed her breasts and pinched her nipples. "Wanna feel?"

He glanced around like he might get in trouble for touching her. "If John hadn't talked to me, convinced me, I'd never be able to do this." He got serious for a second. "I respect you and like you too much to just use you."

Awww. Well... that melted her heart even more. "Aren't you the sweetest young man? But, you see, being used is one of my hot-button triggers." Her curiosity swelled. She wanted to know more about this man with each passing second. "Exactly how old are you, Anderson?"

"I'm twenty-six."

"Wow! I could be your mother!" she exclaimed with a frivolous laugh. She knew he was young, but holy shit.

"I know. That's makes it even hotter for me." His lust was showing more and more on his face, and she adored it.

"Oh, a MILF lover. I see. A very common fantasy. Though I'm not a mom, I could be." This was going to be so delicious. She seriously couldn't contain her excitement. She just wanted his dick on her, in her, coming on her bare flesh.

He nodded his head exaggeratedly. "Yes. Oh, fuck yes, I am, ma'am. Ever since I hit thirteen, I've loved older women. My friend's mom's especially." He reached for her right breast and fondled it as his eyes flared bright with want. "Because I also knew them on a personal level, yet they were sexy as fuck."

She smiled at him, appreciating his desire for an age gap because she shared it.

"Fuck. This is a dream come true." His eyes bulged as he greedily scanned her naked body.

His hesitation disappeared as he roughly grabbed both her breasts and caressed them, his face showing his extreme enjoyment at being able to finally touch her this way. He mashed them between his strong fingers. He was a bit aggressive in his grabbing and it lit her up. When he took to touching and firmly pinching her nipples, she cried out with desire, "Oh, that feels so good, Anderson. Don't stop."

He squeezed her breasts harder yet, and then tugged her nipples away from her body.

She squeaked and squealed as he yanked on them. "Fuck," she exclaimed as if starved for his touch.

"He's really watching us?" Anderson asked breathlessly as he glanced towards the house.

"Yes. He's watching. And probably stroking his dick."

Anderson fluttered his eyelids and looked confused for a second, and concern flitted across his face. "I hadn't thought about that."

"Does it bother you?" she asked, thinking likely it didn't.

He relaxed again and the horniness took over. "No. I just hadn't thought about this that way until you said it." He pulled her into a hug and grinned at her. "I can do this. And, being honest, it actually turns me on more than I expected it would."

"Good," she said.

His erection felt large against her belly as he pressed himself to her.

"Mmmm. I really, really can't wait for your cock to be riding me."

He leaned down and kissed her as his hands meandered down her back. He gripped both her ass cheeks firmly and squeezed them hard, lifting her off the ground slightly.

"Oh, I'm going to ride you, my dear. And hard. Really hard." His voice now so strong and determined, it sent a twitch through her clit.

He was showing the signs of a strong lover who didn't hold back.

She squeaked into their kiss as he ground his cock against her stomach. His hands quickly snuck to her thighs, and he hoisted her up to straddle his middle.

She rapaciously locked her legs around him, raging for more of him.

They kept kissing as he held her up, which seemed to be of very little effort on his part.

He kissed down her neck and she fingered his thick hair. He kept kissing down her chest until he reached her left nipple. He consumed it quickly with a chomping sound and suckled her tit to the back of his throat.

She threw her head back with a moan, writhing slightly in his arms as he feasted on her erect nipple. He chewed it slightly and it pistoned jolts of intense sensations through her torso.

"Oh, fuck," she garbled through gasps. His teeth gnashing her nips so forcefully was a new sensation for her.

He was a very strong man, and his rough touches and sucks thickened her desire for more.

"More, yes, more please," she whispered, barely able to speak as he worked over her peaked pink flesh.

He mauled her with his hands and his mouth. She was dripping wet, anticipating what his cock would do to her pussy, and those lumberjack-looking hips of his.

She was slipping into a reverie of passion when a loud police siren rang out and then began to dim. All the while he was still chomping on her tits. He was hungry for this, and she was ecstatic to be able to feed him.

"Yes, Anderson, oh my gawwwwd," she slurred as he squeezed her thighs and ground his thick dick into her body. "Please, will you fuck me?"

"You are coming first," he growled. He carried her to the lounge chair he'd watched her climax on, and carefully laid her down.

His gentle handling of her came as a bit of shock after his harsh grabs.

"But I did already. I want you to fuck me. I want that dick in me." She sounded whiny and desperate, and she found the humiliation yummy.

"But I haven't made you come yet. You are coming first," he commanded, the lust transforming him from a nervous young man to a horny beast of a full-grown man. His confidence was beyond sexy, and it strengthened her desire to submit to him, to give him her pussy any way he wanted her. It was the most exciting transformation she'd witnessed in one of her hotwifing partners yet. Permission suited this man so very well.

"You are unbelievably sexy, Anderson," she said in a soft but firm voice. "I've been eyeing you up for years now, wishing I could fuck you, and now here we are." Her panting had her breathless.

"Same," he said in a raspy voice. "Spread your legs," he instructed in a commanding tone.

She obeyed immediately. Either John had coached him well, or this was naturally who he was. And both of those prospects were very exciting.

Chapter 3

He stripped all his clothes off so fast she almost would have missed it had she blinked. His cock was thick and looked longer than John's. She wanted it so bad she almost begged for him to put it in her, but she didn't get the chance because he fell to his knees and devoured her waiting cunt in a flash.

"F-f-fuck," she gasped out as he chowed down on her lips. Her head fell back as she succumbed to him pleasuring her.

He went straight in for her clit with his mouth and her slit with his fingers like he knew what he was doing. She was sure John had informed him of what she liked, as he usually did with her partners he set up. This was most evident in how he used strong closed-mouth sucking and aggressive presses of his fingers, then slipped his tongue inside her pussy hole for a tongue fuck. His tongue was so thick and firm.

"Oh, Gawd, yes," she murmured, writhing and shifting her hips up and down.

He tracked her movements like a master, his mouth never leaving her cunt. "Mmmm," he muttered with her muff filling his face. "You taste incredible," he said against her flesh.

She held his head as she writhed against him, eating her out. Her thighs closed on his head and squeezed.

He laughed into her slit, his hot breath and vocal vibrations ramping up her enjoyment.

"Squeeze me all you want. You won't hurt me," he muttered in a muffled voice before taking all her fleshy woman bits back into his mouth. He sucked her clit hard, and she thrashed like a caught fish pinned to the boat floor.

Moans filled the air, and she figured if her neighbor was outside, he was most certainly watching through the hole in the fence. It had appeared one day and neither she nor John had any intention of blocking his peeping activities on them. It only fed their lust to wonder when he was watching. He'd grunted a few times recently when John had fucked her prone doggystyle on the pool stairs, so they knew his eyes were on them. That had been a super-hot fuck session and his likely watching had made it epic. She kept telling John they needed to flat-out invite him over to watch them fuck, but John hadn't granted her request yet.

Without evidence of any hesitation at all, Anderson finger fucked her as he ate her out, and within a few minutes her body was clenching around him as she came hard. The orgasm took her so forcefully that she uttered primal sounds that surprised even herself. If she weren't so overcome with her climaxing, she'd have laughed at herself, sounding like an animal in heat.

He kept sucking her, even as she tried to squirm away because her clit was so sensitive it hurt, but he had her pinned. The next orgasm almost made her want to punch his head for how strong it was. She desperately needed a break from the intensity of it. Her body was rocked by the contractions that took over. She had no control over herself as the orgasm sent wave after wave of pulses through her. He didn't stop there, but kept eating her out until she flat-out screamed.

She turned her head towards the sounds of someone clapping. Through partially closed eyes, she saw it was John standing in front of the sliding door. "Very well done, Anderson."

She forced her eyes to open fully. John looked so proud.

"Proud of you babe, you let him take you there." He took a few steps forward, his eyes glittering with lust. "Now fuck her good with that hard, eager young strong cock of yours, Anderson." He clapped again. "Fuck her hard." It was a non-negotiable command. "I want her fully spent before my turn. Make her a rag doll."

The determined look of pure lust in Anderson's eyes as he penetrated her with his cock sent her skyrocketing toward another climax. He nailed her so hard repeatedly atop the mesh fabric of the chair, she feared he'd jackhammer her right through it.

His cock was thick, and definitely bigger than John's as it stretched her pussy deep and wide. He grunted as he rammed himself into her, and she wished she could have John's view of his ass as he thrust himself vigorously into her.

She writhed and moaned as Anderson obliterated her pussy. She raged into a double-peaked orgasm as he relentlessly banged into her. She came again, hard, and was a quivering mess as she watched her husband approach.

Anderson pulled his cock out of her. "Whew, almost came," he sputtered.

"Fuck her doggy," John demanded. "I want you to rail her."

"Yes, sir," Anderson answered with absolution. "It'd be my deepest pleasure."

She was too floppy to stand so Anderson scooped her up. His handling of her was gentle again. It was such a strong contrast to how he fucked her that it garnered her affections for him further. She needed more of this man in her hotwifing fun.

"Over the woodpile. Fuck her doggy over the wood pile," John said sternly.

'Wow' was the only thought she could muster.

She saw John pull out his phone and ready it to video them. This was titillating and she filled with glee. This was a new level of illicit voyeurism that raged her passion to the max. She was so excited she couldn't stand properly, which was fine because then Anderson pushed her roughly down to lean over the pile of logs and she was supported.

She grunted as he shoved his cock into her, as wet as she was, his gruff entering of her didn't hurt a single bit but forced her closer to another orgasm.

The coarse wood rubbed her flesh as he smashed his cock into her from behind. She came again with such force that she shuddered against the woodpile in a series of full-body twitches.

She squealed and clawed at the wood, wondering how much longer her skin would hold out before it'd be scratched. She didn't want to find out. It was already digging into her abdomen, but it didn't feel like broken skin.

Thankfully, Anderson pulled his cock out, so she was no longer rubbed up against the logs, and his hot cum splatted across her ass and lower back, then a spurt hit her upper back.

She crumpled to the ground, panting and spent, destroyed, and floaty with all the sex hormones saturating her body.

He plucked her off the ground and cradled her in his arms gently, like she was a baby.

"You okay?" he whispered with his eyes full of concern. "That was so hot, but I got rougher than I meant to."

She stared into his eyes with hers, soft yet full of zest. "It was incredible. One of the best of my life, Anderson." And John played a major role in that. She glanced at John. He was grinning so big. She found it so arousing that he got carried away and got more aggressive. "Honestly, I loved your passion." She stroked his face.

"That was outstanding, Anderson. And I got it on video. Do you mind?" John looked really happy.

"Not at all." He chuckled heartily. With a sheepish grin, he asked, "Can I have a copy? And don't share my face with others."

"Of course not," John said seriously. "Okay. I'll send it to you now."

"Thank you. Thank you both. That was one of the best fucks of my life too." He licked his lips as he looked her in the eyes. "Because I already had a friendship with you, and cause I find you so attractive. Your adventurous spirit is a huge turn-on as well."

"Agreed," she whispered.

He was still holding her in his arms. He looked John in the eyes and walked towards him before transferring her to John's waiting arms.

"Can't thank you guys enough." He rubbed his temples. "I suppose I'd better get to working on your pool. I still have several other houses to hit today before I'm done."

"Yeah, thanks, Anderson." John cuddled her and their foreheads touched. He turned his full attention to her. "I'm going to fuck you now. Your choice. In front of Anderson or alone?"

Her eyes twinkled with her answer before she said it. "In front of Anderson." Her mind reeled as she wondered where this whole introduction of swinging with Anderson might go. Maybe they'd DV fuck her next time, or maybe spit roast her. However it might happen, she instantly wanted them to both fuck her at once.

"Good girl," John said appreciatively. "Aw, Anderson, before you get to work, would you like to watch me fuck Laney? Or watch as you work if you want."

Anderson stopped in his tracks and spun around as if he were on ice. "Fuck yes, I'd love to watch. Want me to video you two?"

The excitement of that surged inside her and as cum-drunk as she was, her passion exploded even more. "Fuck me, John. Please fuck me in front of Anderson. Now. Please." She wanted to say it too because hearing herself say the words was exciting and satisfying.

"Yes, babe. My good girl," he said in a firm voice.

He carried her to the grass and laid her face down in it. The blades slid along her skin like soft little plush fingers. She heard him unzip his pants and then felt him kneel between her spread thighs. He brushed his cockhead along her slit and slipped right inside her wet pussy. He began to fuck her slow at first, her body chugging along the plush lawn, then he rammed himself into her harder and harder, his grunting and groans alone driving her to the point of almost climaxing.

He leaned down and stopped his thrusting into her. His breath was hot on her ear. She shuddered with eagerness. He whispered in her ear, "Do you have the strength to go on your hands-and-knees, baby?"

She nodded against the grass, though she wasn't sure that she did, but she wanted Anderson to see her tits swing wildly as John fucked her from behind. Plus, she also hoped to look into Anderson's eyes as she got fucked, just as she had when John fucked her in front of Jaxon.

She wearily pulled herself to a hands-and-knees position. She was shaking from weakness and enthusiasm. Immediately she was thrilled because Anderson had moved to about six feet in front of them and was stroking his hardon with one hand while filming them with John's phone with the other.

"Mmmm, fuck that's hot," she said as she held eye contact with Anderson.

He held her gaze with a libidinous grin. Bless him.

John pressed his hard cock into her and began to rock her body with his hard thrusts. Her tits swung violently as he fucked her savagely, making her ass cheeks shake. John reached around for titty grabs, then pressed her clit with his fingers. He rode her clit hard, and she slammed into another orgasm. Her body jerked as she curled to the ground.

"That's right, head down, ass up, my cumslut," John commanded brusquely.

He fucked her ruthlessly with her ass pointed up, her face rubbing grass. Before long, he came inside her pussy in a wet gush of his cum.

"Oh, fuck," he muttered as he continued to pump his softening cock into her fuckhole. "Fuck, that was so good. Damn!" he exclaimed. "Whew!" he shouted to the sky.

Hearing his exuberance was so satiating as she collapsed to the ground. He sat next to her. He was panting excessively as he pulled her upper body into his lap and held her, dropping a kiss on the top of her head.

"Epic fuck, babe. That was incredible. I'm soaring now. Shit!" He kept panting as he grinned.

She opened her eyes fully as Anderson spoke. "Came again. That was unbelievably hot. Guys, wow. Thanks for letting me watch."

"That's part of the excitement for us too," John admitted.

"Damn, I hope I marry a woman as sexually open as you someday, Laney. You're amazing, like off the charts incredible." He put his cock back into his pants. "It was like living in porn."

"She is amazing. So amazing. I don't deserve her. But I know I'm a very lucky man. But I didn't realize how lucky until recently, when we really started opening up." He pressed his lips together. "I used to be a selfish ass."

"Aww, Daddy," she said with affection.

"Well, I loved it." Anderson jostled his dick in his shorts. "Fuck," he stammered. He shook his head as he scoffed. "Getting hard again."

"Wow, nice. I remember those days well," John said with chagrin.

"Hey. Anytime you need extra work done like that, text me. I'll come immediately." He laughed nervously.

"Definitely young man. We would love that, I'm guessing, right, Laney?"

"Oh, fuck yes. In fact, maybe next time you can both fuck me at once? Please?" She begged with her eyes, desperately hoping John would take her suggestion.

They each let out a burst of laughter.

"Yeah, baby, we can do that. You in, Anderson?"

"Oh, hell yes, I am. I still can't believe what just happened. I think I'm kind of in shock."

"Good shock, I hope?" John asked as he hugged her tighter.

"Yes, well, I'd better get to work. Do you have a cup of water though? I'm a bit parched."

"Yes, go into the basement and grab one from the bar fridge. Help yourself to as many as you need." John rocked her back and forth in his lap. Once Anderson was in the house, John said, "I think we may have found a play partner for the future too. What do you think?"

"Oh, definitely. I'd really love that." She was so happy she could burst. "That was really incredible. I wasn't kidding. It was a dream come true. And I loved the addition of the videoing too, by the way. That was so hot!"

"Yeah, it just hit me." He caressed her face. "I'll text him later to set up another date."

"You are the best husband in the world. How did I get this lucky?" she asked in a soothing voice.

"I could say the same thing, babe." They kissed on the lips. "Hmmm. I suppose I'd better get back to work too so I can be done by dinner."

"Yup. And I planned to get the laundry done before I cook. Want to finish up that movie tonight with dinner?"

"Yeah, babe. That sounds perfect."

She lounged in the grass soaking up the sun as John went back into the house. She waited for Anderson to come out, but he wasn't coming. She grinned because this confirmed it for her, the men were talking about the next fuck date. She couldn't wait! She pondered asking John if they could create an account to post the video, but they'd have to edit out Anderson's face. This was a secret yearning she had to be a sexual content creator, but would John go for it too?

She remained in the yard naked. It was a hundred percent surety that at least one of the neighbors must have looked out by now and saw her sprawled out nude. The question was ... had they seen any of the sex? No police car siren was approaching, so she figured they were safe thus far. Was it illegal to be naked and fucking in one's own yard? She wasn't sure. She didn't care, but she didn't want any trouble either.

After about fifteen minutes both John and Anderson emerged. Both men looked extremely happy.

"Laney, do you want sunscreen on your tits and pussy? You don't want to get burned," John said with concern.

"No, you are right. But I'm going in anyhow." She stood up and enjoyed Anderson's appreciative expression.

"I have good news, Laney. Anderson has agreed to be our bull." John looked much more pleased than she'd expected about such a thing.

"Wow! Seriously?" She jumped and clapped her hands like a cheerleader.

"Yes, and please do that again," John said.

She loved that they'd talked about him fucking her again. Anderson was someone who turned her on and this was going to be so incredible. "I'm beyond excited about this." She rushed up to Anderson and they embraced.

He kissed her and John snuggled up to her backside. Both men held her, and they moved back and forth in a rocking motion.

"When?" she asked breathlessly. She wasn't afraid to admit she could go again.

"This weekend. He will come over Saturday. We will do drinks, appetizers, and feed him dinner. Then we will fuck." John had a plan, and she was so excited they'd plotted. And it was sexy they'd done it out of earshot of her.

"Oh, yay! I will start planning the menu!"

"She's an excellent chef, Anderson. Come hungry!"

"Yes, sir."

They released her and the three went their separate ways.

The rest of the afternoon she periodically peeked out at Anderson as he worked on cleaning the pool, adding chemicals, and pulling weeds. She couldn't stop staring, admiring his sexy body and reminiscing about his gruff hands all over her, his thick cock riding her, and her body climaxing against his. It was such a good day she didn't think they'd ever top it again.

But then ... there was Saturday.

Anderson, The Pool service Man Turned Bull

Book 3

Chapter 1

Laney raised her top half out of the tub. The hot water was a bit too hot, and she needed a few moments to cool down. She smiled deeply as John appeared with a glass of white wine. "For you, my love," he said with a pleasant expression, looking distinguished and sexy, with a bit more gray above his right ear.

Laney noted his cock was already nice and full. She intentionally stared at his crotch and asked, "Do I get what's in there before Anderson arrives? Or do I have to wait?"

He smirked and caressed her cheek. "You will have to wait, my love."

She pouted. "But you love me satiated, and I'm horny."

"Yes, true." He sat on the edge of the tub, his fresh, sea-breezy cologne wafting off his body. "But I also love you edged." His smile was knowing and full of secrets.

"When do I get to know ... anything ... about tonight?" She knew her tone was coming out impatient and bratty, but that was sort of the point. She wanted to twist him to her will, as she so often did.

"All in good time, baby. First things first. I want you freshly bathed and relaxed. Don't worry about a thing. You've got dinner prepped and now you are getting ready for Anderson to come fuck you. That's all you need to do." He patted her head like she was a dog. "Now, enjoy that wine and soak that pussy. Pamper her, because she's going to take a massive pounding in a short while." He smiled so big that she couldn't protest.

She wanted that badly.

Being a hotwife, with John in control, has satiated them both on a level she hadn't thought possible. Him admitting his neglect of her and apologizing had been the first step. At times, she was shocked she did this with John at all, and even more flabbergasted that she loved it.

He also had come to love helping her doll up for sex dates. It was like he was packaging her up in a sexy way for the man who would fuck her, but it was for Laney, too. She loved looking sexy, it made her feel sexier. Not that she was an object, not that she would ever be okay with truly only being a sex object, but yet she loved being objectified and desired for just sex. It was an odd mix she wasn't sure she even understood of herself. But she couldn't deny its existence. She didn't need a psychology degree. She just knew it all made her come like neverending waterfalls.

"Thank you for the wine, lover." She took a sip and gave him her feelings of lust and appreciation on full blast in her gaze up at him.

"You are a gorgeous beauty in this tub. I have plans, but I might be changing them. You look like a delicious sex goddess in that tub." He stroked her arm, then reached to give her right nipple some loving touches.

"Oh, do tell?" Laney coaxed.

"Nope. I'm still formulating." He'd become a true stag to her vixen. John stood up and pulled his cock out. "Suck the tip."

With a wine-coated mouth, she set her glass down and positioned herself on her knees in the tub. Her breasts swung as she shimmied her shoulders.

"Might need a titty fuck now, too." He grinned down at her, his erect cock red and purplish, packed to the brim with blood.

She attacked his cock head with her mouth and rapidly pumped her orifice up and down while alternating between stroking his shaft and balls. She knew he'd be edging, sporting a raging, never fully waning erection, for hours before he'd actually fuck her. The blowjob was a courting dance to their end-of-day fuck, which also included Anderson railing her into a multitude of orgasms while John directed the show. Laney at least knew the skeleton of the date.

He handed her the waterproof G spot toy and said, "Put this in while you suck my cock, but don't you come yet." He was stern.

He grabbed his phone as he groaned. He took a step back so his cock would fall out of her mouth. "Whew, gotta slow the fuck down." He smirked sheepishly. "You are too damn sexy. I need to be done with that. Keep the toy in. I'm going downstairs to keep working on preparations for Anderson's arrival. I'll be pleasuring you from down there." He zipped up his pants and waved his phone at her. "Obey me. Don't come."

"I won't, Daddy. I promise." It was foreign for him to tell her not to come. He was usually trying to get her to climax as many times as her body could handle.

He waved and blew her a kiss, then disappeared around the corner.

She sank back into the tub and took a sip of wine. Life hadn't looked like it would end up like this. In fact, the big D had been a permanent structure in her brain, but she was loving her new version. She wouldn't return to how things were before for anything.

The toy's strength flared, and she lurched forward, almost spilling her wine.

"Holy fuck," she muttered.

"Don't come," John hollered from the floor below.

"Easier said than done, my lovely man." She grinned with humility. He knew how to push her buttons; he'd become the master to the instrument of her pussy. But it had taken some time, and trust. She glanced at the sexy dress he had picked out for her to wear. He'd gotten so into creating her sexpot image, even taking to choosing outfits, shoes, lingerie, and jewelry. She loved it all. It was like he was pampering her with all the attention, and it was the secret sauce that had been missing from their marriage. Well, that and about a hundred other things.

She loved the low-cut red dress and wondered how long it would realistically stay on her body. Not that it mattered. The plan was that she'd cook for the three of them while the men chilled out. She wanted to pamper them this way and had said so when John had offered to help with dinner. Food prep had become her passion, as had the presentation of it. She couldn't get enough of the new exploration and had considered even creating a cookbook of romantic dinner ideas, complete with sex acts to go along with them. She hadn't told John her idea yet, but with his new attitude, she suspected he would be cheering her along on the sidelines. The impression of him perhaps being that way was exciting in and of itself.

The toy's peak was pulsed through her vagina again and she moaned out, slapping her right hand to the side of the tub with a smack. This was going to be very hard to prevent climaxing if he kept this up. But she was up for the challenge. It meant she'd be a raging inferno of a cougar to come when Anderson came to play.

Images of Anderson working in their backyard spilled into her brain as her husband fluctuated the pulses of the toy inside her. His bulging flannel shirts, his stretched t-shirts, and his lovely man ass encased in tight jeans all raged her libido. The man was sexy on a level few men were. He was strong, yet polite, and had fucked her to rag doll status over the wood pile to a level her desire hadn't even dreamt was possible. He was the kind of man who could fuck a woman like a whore and cradle her like a newly bloomed flower. And he easily transformed between the two, slick as ice cubes on water. John had a level of that these days too, but it was rawer and purer in Anderson, with the zest and the crystalline energy of youth. Likely it was just his nature as well; he'd make a very good dominant of his own. But in her experience, most youngsters were too selfish to broach that level of masculine sexual mastery in their early years.

She pressed her now swollen clit, remembering how Anderson had railed her over the rough logs while John had filmed them. What could possibly top that combination of aggressive raw lust and blissful exhibitionistic satiation? Laney wasn't sure, but she was more than ready to find out.

The toy stopped buzzing her. Then she got a text.

It was from John.

John: Take a selfie of yourself in the tub and send it to me and to Anderson.

Oh! She liked this part of the game. She proceeded to pose and took ten selfie pictures of her face and body, close-ups of her nipples and pussy, and one of her ass in the water. This act alone thickened her arousal as she sent both the men her pics.

A half a minute later, John texted back.

John: Good girl.

She surged with his approval. When Anderson texted back, she desperately wanted to rub one out in the tub.

Anderson texted: OMG Sweet sexy baby! You are delicious! I can't wait to come and fuck you into oblivion. Thank you for sharing! My cock is a fat rod and already leaking for you.

She smiled with saucy glee. Both her current men were so wonderful. Full of sexy compliments, encouragement for her, and focused on her pleasure.

She shook her head, remembering. The thoughts crept in at the worst time sometimes. Her life had become such a far cry from her past that she felt she must be living in an alternate universe. Who knew jealousy could turn into this? It literally seemed the opposite. Maybe it was just a miracle, and she should just stop fucking analyzing it and just enjoy. She knew she could most certainly do that. Peas fit in a pod, but only if the pod grew with the peas. She needed to adjust her thinking. With her and John, they most certainly had morphed into the hotwife way of life. Sexual liberation and freedom was glorious!

John appeared in the doorway wearing a robe and a pair of slacks. He appeared to be bare-chested under the robe. He held a cigar in one hand and a whiskey in the other. "Time to dress, babe."

She bit her lip. "Looking like that, I'd like to bounce on your cock on the bed for a bit. Do we have time?"

He shook his head. "Nope." He took a sip of his drink and pointed at his phone. "He will be arriving soon."

The words made her giddy and wanton. The promise Anderson's arrival held filled her up to almost bursting. She rose out of the water and John set down his things to wrap her up in a big fluffy towel.

"Curl your hair today?" he asked hopefully as he dried off her body, taking extra time to snug the plush towel into all her wet cracks.

"Yes, I will. Sure." She'd need a fair amount of time for that. His request warmed her.

"I'll refresh your wine. Be right back."

He had taken to full-service caretaking of her before sex dates. It had worked on fattening up their intimacy more than she'd expected. He wanted her feeling amazing, well fucked, luxuriously fed, and floaty from orgasms. He not only took action to bring this about, but he also told her he wanted all that. She was so lucky she pinched herself. Who was this new version of John anyway? And what fairy godmother had done the magic to turn him into it? She celebrated it with the utmost delight however it came about.

She covered her skin in floral body butter, then scrunched her hair with Moroccan argan oil. She dried it while naked to let the lotion soak in. Then she added more curls with the curling iron.

John appeared with her glass of wine and, after setting it on the counter, he fitted his erection to nestle between her still bare buttocks. "Wow, you smell and look so sexy and delicious. You are going to drive Anderson wild." He thrust his cock against her crack.

"Mmmm," she muttered. "I sure hope so. I'm feeling very plump with want myself. I'd really love to have more of your cock right now, though," she begged openly. "Please?"

He chuckled as he swayed her body from behind. "No, babe. You can not have my cock yet. After I'm done with directing you and Anderson. Only then can you enjoy my meat."

She pouted with a fat lip and sad eyes. "Meanie."

He squeezed her bottom hard, and she squealed and went up on her tippy toes. "I'm so mean, I know. Now, get ready for Anderson's big dick. I'll be downstairs waiting for him." He gave her a swat on the butt before slipping away.

She stuffed her desire down a bit so she wouldn't be tempted to scramble to the bed with a sex toy and launch herself into a big O. It certainly wouldn't take much in her current state. Her lust had been sufficiently, and overly, ignited.

She primped her hair, then slinked the tight dress on. Carefully putting on makeup gave her a new focus and she settled down off the raging hormonal high. She adorned herself with John's chosen jewelry and prepared to head downstairs. She snatched her new sex toy from the bedside table. It was a deliciously curved, realistic-looking dildo about the size of John's cock, so he'd appropriately named it 'Daddy's Cock', or DC for short. She loved it and wanted to show it to Anderson. She planned to tell him it was John's cock, and she wanted him to fuck her with it. She grinned suggestively as she slid it into her snug cleavage with the cock tip peeping out.

She descended the stairs and heard the men talking and laughing like they were having a good time. She relished that they got along and enjoyed each other's company. John was clearly curating Anderson into the kind of bull who would eagerly satisfy her, but it seemed to be coming so perfectly naturally to Anderson. They were all just the right fit for their kinky triad.

Threesomes had always turned Laney on, but John had always refused to try it out, unless it had been a woman, but their relationship had just never manifested that. She was fine with that. This was better.

She entered the room and both men's eyes fell upon her. Their gazes were both lit with a healthy dose of lust, which made Laney quiver with anticipation. She still held onto the dream of them both fucking her at once. She'd told John this, but he hadn't shown interest. But then he liked to surprise her too, so that may have been intentional.

"Wow, holy fuck, you look beyond amazing! Sexy sexy sexy," Anderson said with a voice full of arousal. He licked the corner of his lip. "I can't wait to fuck you, Laney." He guffawed. "And I can't believe I get to say that in front of your husband."

"The more you say to her the better," John said with full encouragement. "You look so sexy as fuck, Laney. I can't wait to fuck you, either. You are going to be a mush pile of sex hormones once we are done with you." John growled. "Now get over here, whore."

She dashed to the couch with a devilish grin and sat on the couch between the two men, right where John patted.

"Place that sexy little butt right here." His hand went right to her knee. "I see your breasts are hugging an adornment. I think another cock needs to be there though"

She giggled. "Yep. Your cock." She pulled it out and presented it to Anderson. "This is Daddy's Cock. DC for short. I want you to fuck me with Daddy's Cock."

Anderson's eyes lit up. "Oh! I get to rail you with this too? This just keeps getting better!" Anderson was dressed in a nice bright blue polo shirt and a pair of tight jeans. He looked so different from the rugged Anderson, who'd always showed up to service the pool or do manual labor. She couldn't wait for the fall when he'd be showing up at the house in those sexy flannels again.

She popped the corner of his collar up. "Nice shirt. It matches your sexy eyes."

"Thank you. John asked me to dress up. I guess this is as dressed up as I get." He looked confident rather than sheepish and apologetic, which was a turn-on to Laney.

"Well, I love it. And I'm glad we are dressed this way." She glanced at her husband in his robe and slacks and secretly loved the casual yet managerial flair of his outfit. It was like he was playing the billionaire boyfriend, lounging and savoring life, getting all the sex he wanted, and boasting because of it. This was also a turn-on because he was giving Laney exactly what she wanted, while taking what she offered because he wanted it as well.

"I need to start the dinner prep, but do either of you need another beverage?" She smiled coquettishly at the men, hoping to serve them. Those who served her got served back. It was only logical and actually was quite satisfying.

They both indicated interest in another cocktail, and she zoomed off to the kitchen.

The men moved outside to sit on the patio as she played bartender, making them each a whiskey sour. She danced seductively to the rock music streaming from her phone and her soul breathed free. The sunshine was generous and piled itself into the windows in a brilliant blaze. She couldn't help but desire to dance about in it, naked in the backyard, with both men lusting after her. If there was one thing she loved, it was turning men on, then being ravaged by them. She'd courted with the idea of a gangbang, but that was something she was keeping to herself for the moment. Many would see that as the ultimate in being used, but that was a kink in and of itself. The number of orgasms she'd likely get from one blew her mind. She knew it would be off the charts. That all excited her massively.

No matter. This was a legit fantasy, too. Getting to fuck Anderson again was a monumental fantasy.

She grabbed two beef sticks and plopped them in the drinks before flitting down the stairs as if her body were a feather. She floated outside and placed the drinks in front of both. They each grabbed for her ass, one hand per cheek. They both felt her up, each of their hands staying on their claimed ass cheek. She adored that their first instinct was to touch her in some way.

She soaked up the attention as their cigar smoke wafted up. The scent of the cigars induced a mood in Laney of indulgence and relaxation, even though she didn't like smoking. Both their faces looked as happy as she felt. It was going to be a very good evening.

Chapter 2

The summer sounds were bliss as Laney bent over the patio table from John's push. She laid her ample bosom on the wrought iron metal as both of them felt up her ass. John's fingers explored further towards her pussy, meandering gently between her folds. His touch was arousing, and it amplified when Anderson's large fingers joined the pressing party of her pussy. She moaned and writhed into their sexual touching. John led the way to her clit, and Anderson's fingers followed. They both circled her clit, pressed it, and took turns rubbing it.

Fuck. She was gigantically turned on by them touching her this way when all of them were dressed and supposed to be being proper, sitting on the patio. She might climax from this alone.

She gasped when, first, John's fingers entered her pussy, then again as Anderson's followed. They both finger fucked her slow then rapid as her panting and moans increased. This was wildly unexpected and deliciously outrageous to be finger fucked in broad daylight over a table by two men she found organically sexy.

Their jabs aroused her internal erectile sponge, molesting her G spot to a provocative level. When John placed his thumb upon her clit, she cried out.

He immediately pulled his fingers out of her cunt; Anderson followed suit.

She lay untouched with her dress up over her exposed ass, panting on the metal table, the sun toasting her skin.

"Oh, my gawd," she said through excessive panting.

"I think we'd better slow things down a bit." John sounded authoritarian.

Laney was beginning to hate that phrase.

"Why?" she asked in a whiny voice.

"Because I don't want to take the glory out of later."

She stood up, not bothering to fix her mussed-up dress so both men could full-on see her bare pussy. "That's just not fair."

John snickered as she stomped off into the house.

What the hell was he doing? This wasn't his usual plan. He loved to make her climax on repeat and break the numbers barrier. And now he was stopping?

And when she was so hot, she'd have come right on their fingers for any onlookers to see? She was just confused, and, too, John's almost mocking of her ticked her off.

She huffed herself up the stairs and glanced around the kitchen, trying to placate her turned-on brain. There was work to be done for the meal, so perhaps she should thank John because, even if she had come, she'd have wanted to again. Breaking the orgasm seal was a hard phenomenon to cap off. No matter. She'd enjoy the hell of her orgasms later, when they both fucked her.

She coated her throat with wine again and began to compile the salad. She'd prepped it earlier and now it was an easy and quick put-together. Her anger raged, though, at being their toy to edge.

She stopped herself and laughed out loud. Wait a minute. This is exactly what she wanted! To be edged and teased so much that her orgasm was as explosive as possible. She couldn't be mad at John for that. He was following his own plan of making her come as hard as possible. She just hadn't expected to be pushed that far and then had her impending orgasm ruined. It had felt like a huge one looming too, so she lamented the loss of it.

John appeared with an amused look. "I'm sorry, baby. I didn't mean to make you mad. Are you okay?"

She laughed at herself. "I really got mad, didn't I?"

"You did. Wanted to check on you." He pulled her into a hug and kissed the top of her head. "I only want the biggest pleasures for you. Maybe I should have let you have that one. I'm pretty stuck on my plan, but I know I need to be flexible and spontaneous, too."

"Yeah," she pouted, but then smiled up at him because he was saying all the right stuff. She kissed him on the lips. "It seemed like a monster O was coming. It was so unexpected and yummy to have you two start touching me like that. I guess it launched me."

"Ah, that is a bummer. Damn. But don't you worry. We are going to make you scream on repeat from so much orgasmic pleasure you might fall into a sex coma."

She grinned. "Forgiven. Now, will you help me carry out this salad? I'll bring napkins, forks, and bread. I have to put the salmon in the oven, and I'll be right out to join you two."

He released her after another kiss. "You are my priority, Laney. Don't forget that. And I'm going to prove that to you every day for the rest of our lives." He grabbed for the salad as she handed him the bowls. Lastly, he snatched her glass of wine and made his way back to Anderson via the sliding door to the deck. He winked at her before he turned. "It's a promise."

His words comforted and excited her. She wanted all of that, which was not something she could have said before their current way of life. She turned on some festive pop music on her phone and then set about putting the finishing touches of butter, fresh cilantro leaves, sea salt, and lime slices to the salmon. She bent over and popped it in the oven. The sheer act of bending over brought back the thoughts of what had just happened on the patio table. Whew! It was time to get this night going.

She kept her music playing as she descended the deck stairs, the light summer evening breeze lifting her locks and caressing her bare skin as she moved. She felt lovely and the night matched her. It was a fabulous night to get fucked outside.

"Thank you, John." He had served up the salad into the three bowls. "Looks perfect."

They all settled around the table. This time Laney sat beside Anderson, and across from John. She kept glancing backward, so John motioned for her to come sit next to him.

"This may not be as conducive to conversation, but I want you to enjoy the backyard view, too."

"Thank you. That's a great idea." She moved all her stuff to sit beside John, and he moved her wine glass.

"Busy day today, Anderson?" John was in a jovial mood, even though his question was more serious.

"It was, yes. I had an extra house to visit today, so I had nine." He shoved a huge fork full of salad into his mouth and chewed like a hungry man.

Laney instantly desired to fulfill all his appetites, every last dirty, filthy, dark, and taboo fantasy. She'd have a total fucking blast doing it, acting out all the parts, but she'd need John present for the trust factor as master overseer. She trusted Anderson, having known him for years, but she needed that comfort of full intimate trust. John would be the turnkey for that.

"I'm going to get the shrimp cocktail. I'll be right back." Laney rose from the table and walked off, looking back to see if they were watching her butt as she walked. She felt warm fuzzies as she caught both their eyes roaming her body.

"Need help, babe?" John asked with a cock of his head.

"No, it's already ready. I just need to pull it out of the fridge."

When she returned, she set the tray down. Anderson grabbed her hand and pulled her onto his lap. His eyes were warm as melted chocolate and his cock beneath her bottom was hard as cement. He cradled her to him, gazed into her eyes while holding her cheeks, then kissed her deeply. They made out with her squirming on his lap as John kept smoking.

"Mmmmm," John muttered. "You two are turning me on."

Laney could have slid down his cock and rode him to an orgasm in no time, but her phone's timer went off. "Oh, damn. The salmon is done." Laney leaned to slide off Anderson's lap.

John stood. "Allow me."

"Oh, I'll come too. I have to get the other things as well." Laney tried to quell her lust again, but it wasn't working so well.

"Need another set of hands?" Anderson asked, starting to rise from his chair.

"I think we can get it, Anderson. You sit tight and enjoy," Laney said graciously.

In the kitchen, John waited patiently as Laney pulled the salmon from the oven. Then he whirled her into his arms and kissed her in a strong, open-mouthed kiss, twining her tongue with his.

"I want you so bad, Laney. I can't wait to fuck you once you are a rotten wet hot mess from Anderson ravishing you."

"Same," she said as she slithered her body against his, ensuring a press of her abdomen against his hard cock.

They kissed for a few more minutes and could have easily fucked right there on the kitchen island, but John pulled back from her.

"We are getting carried away. Let's bring the food down and eat."

She nodded in agreement. Her libido couldn't take much more of this tease. She was ready to tackle one, or both men, and seduce them into having sex. She knew just how she'd succeed, too, but that would ruin John's plan, so she reined her desire in.

She focused her brain on what was at hand, and that was dinner. "Right," she muttered. "Potato salad, beans, and pasta salad." She handed John the potato salad. "I'll bring the rest. I need to transfer the beans and salmon to fresh dishes that aren't hot."

Out on the patio, Anderson was looking like a male calendar centerfold as he lounged with an ankle propped up on his knee. His lush hair was slightly windblown, and his plush lips were full and perky as he pressed them together after blowing out cigar smoke. His cheeks held a rosy tinge, which made him look even more virile and irresistible.

Laney licked her lips. The taste of cigar had been on both their tongues. She liked the smell of them, but not the taste. "Ready to eat? I made a mountain of food." She settled into her chair. "I made angel food with strawberries and whipped cream for dessert."

"You're the dessert," Anderson said quickly, with a wicked grin.

"I sure hope so!" Laney retorted with pleasure.

"Can't thank you enough for ensuring you are clean, Anderson. Now we can all enjoy the evening worry-free."

"Oh, it's my pleasure, sir." He scooped up several filets of salmon onto his plate.

"Take more. I only want one piece. And it's not that great as a leftover, so eat up." She grinned at him. She really liked feeding him, and this was the first time she'd gotten to. A man needed fuel to fuck like a beast.

"Okay, I won't argue with the chef!" He helped himself to two more. "And I've come to a decision. I'm going to be your bull and only your bull, while you'll have me, if you'll want me, that is, until I find the woman of my dreams." He stared right at Laney. "Other than Laney." He chuckled to show it was a joke, but his eyes told her he was serious.

"Seriously? My young man, that makes me very happy to hear. We'd love that scenario, and if you want to join in more, we'd love to have you around the house more, right, Laney?"

"Oh, most definitely. I'd love to have you coming around more, Anderson. As much as you want, really." Her libido and her imagination skyrocketed. She couldn't wait for more of Anderson! Him around the house more meant she'd get fucked even more. More of his cock, more of his thrust, more of his targeted sexual confidence and assertiveness. Yes, please! He was a very horny man with a very strong sex drive. And that thrilled her to the max.

"Following your rules and boundaries and approval, of course. I wouldn't just show up, sir, unless you were okay with it."

"Well, I'm open to you pleasuring her anytime, but let's stay in frequent open communication. I'm here most days anyhow, so I'd be around if you came over. I like to watch over her and take on the role of her leader and caretaker in all sexual situations, and otherwise."

Anderson nodded profusely as he chewed. "Of course, sir. I completely understand and respect that."

Laney could fly into the sky like dandelion puffs with how elated this new development made her. She'd get Anderson, the sexy lumberjack of a sex machine on a regular basis. Life could not get any better than that. She beamed a ginormous smile at both of them.

John laughed, delighted. "Well, look how happy you've made my wife, and your cock hasn't even graced her pussy yet." He slapped his thigh several times. "This will be an excellent collaboration indeed."

Laney had a million questions erupting in her head. How kinky was Anderson, really? Did he like restraint? Impact play? Would he allow John's cock to slide along his in a double vaginal sex session? Would John allow that? What would Anderson be interested in role-playing with her? She couldn't wait to find it all out.

Laney considered John. He'd been open to more new sexual things these days. But not all men would be down with their cock sliding along another man's. It would take a very special and open set of men for such a scenario. Laney knew she could keep dreaming of it, regardless. It was good fantasy fodder for her alone playtime.

She squirmed in her seat, suddenly not hungry, but very horny.

John put a hand on her arm. "Let's eat first so you don't get lightheaded, baby."

He knew her so well. She needed to eat, or she wouldn't be in a good head space. "Yes, I know. I'm just really excited."

Anderson and John nodded, and both snickered. Sex with both of them was going to be epic. Her head spun with ideas and questions. Where would they fuck? Would it be outside? Where would John hide this time? Would they video again? Would John agree to posting it somewhere online for others to watch? Would Anderson? Would she get fucked by Anderson tomorrow and the next day too? How often would he come over?

She gobbled her food as she sat silently. The men discussed sports teams she didn't care about. Her mind was filled with sex, not the frivolities of sports teams winning or losing, or who was drafted to which team. All that shit didn't matter squat to Laney.

She watched Anderson eat. It was quite sexy to watch him enjoying food so much. She imagined his mouth upon her nipples, sucking her nips hard to the back of his throat, then him nibbling her erect nubby flesh. She fantasized about his mouth traveling her body, him eating at her cunt the way he ate food, and her desire for that almost made her hop out of her chair and rush over to him. She'd entice him with her body and give it to him to satiate himself. She wanted to feel his strong thrusting, the robust veins on his cock riding her clit, her lower lips, and her G spot. She snuck a hand down to her pussy and confirmed she was already wet as a lubed-up sex toy.

She'd need to snatch DC from the living room before they started. The problem was, she didn't know when or where they would start. That was in John's brain. And likely in Anderson's, since they'd talked awhile before she joined them. She was one hundred percent certain John had already briefed Anderson on the plan for the sex.

They finished eating and both men told Laney they'd clean up. John set her up poolside with another glass of wine.

"Take a swim if you want. We won't be long."

She smirked. "I wanted to fuck hours ago, at salad time, and I barely made it through dinner. 'Long' is way overdue." She made light of it, but it was no joke. She was desperate to get fucked, and get fucked right then, right there. Her libido had it with the waiting and she considered stripping to force them to take her. Maybe she'd strip and bend over and present her ass high in the air so that when they came out, they'd have to fuck her. She knew she was being an impatient sex hangry brat, but maybe if she played her cards right, they'd teach her a lesson and rail the absolute shit out of her like the sluttiest whore on the planet.

She watched them be gallant and take all the dishes in, all the while pining for their cocks to be riding her cum drenched cunt instead. She groaned as she considered touching herself. No. she'd wait. She wanted her climax to be with them.

"Phooey!" she shouted to the warm sky. The shout at least released some of her pent-up energy, but not nearly enough.

Chapter 3

Anderson emerged out of the sliding door looking very much like he belonged poolside in palm tree patterned swim trunks. He was carrying a pair of goggles that also covered up the nose. Seeing him mostly naked in her state of mega horniness was agonizing. Why weren't they fucking her yet? This was supposed to be a fuck date, after all. She released a quick breath in frustration.

"John told me to take a quick dip while he finished up." He was so fresh-faced and happy she couldn't complain, but inside her brat mode was quickly making her as rabid as a ravenous boar. His body was perfectly sculpted. He would be the top choice to pose for a sculptor. She figured he must lift weights too with how contoured his body was. No wonder he had such power when fucking. The man looked like a fuck god. A gilded sex machine. She sighed as her pussy twitched, and her libido screamed at her.

He slipped into the water with a sigh. "Oh, that feels good."

She knew something else that would feel better. She almost snorted out loud. His cock up her pussy.

He swam about in the water for several minutes, glancing her way every so often, as if he wasn't a bit hot for her at all. Laney was confused as to why he hadn't asked her to join him. She was perplexed about why he wasn't attacking her like a bull with a bulging hard-on. She was willing meat, wanton in fact. And where was John? She bit her lower lip and told herself to chill out. This didn't need to be rushed. Her impatience might amuse John, but it was driving her batshit fucking ass crazy.

Anderson swam about doing the front crawl, the backstroke, and the breaststroke. Laney watched his body work practically drooling. She was bursting at the seams to scream 'fuck me already'.

She couldn't take it anymore and finally said in an entitled tone, "Alright, what's going on here? I thought we were fucking on this date." She knew she sounded like a spoiled little hotwife, but seriously, this was getting ridiculous. She had been promised wild abandon and relentless pounding sex and she was just standing poolside like a volleyball net pole.

Anderson kept a straight face and made his way to her side of the pool. He propped his muscular arms up on the edge and gazed at her with too much control when what she wanted was for him to lose control and fuck her to a cummy pulp.

"Want to swim with me?"

To Laney, that didn't sound like a sexy invite at all. She drew in a deep long breath and then released it fast. "Does it involve fucking?"

"No."

That's it? That's all he was going to say? She was ready to run into the house and demand to know John's plan because this shit was worthless. She was ready to demand dick from both of them.

His face turned amused as he said, "You don't need a swimsuit. Come on in. Join me. The water feels incredible."

Well, that sounded a little better. She felt her body relax a tiny bit. But it wasn't enough. She huffed and stuffed her arms under her breasts. "I'll come in if you fuck me in the pool." She couldn't understand why she was so gripped by this impatience. It was as if she'd never been fucked in her life.

She watched him watch her and remained silent as her temper boiled. "Well?" she demanded.

He pushed himself back from the wall and kicked his way to the other side of the pool with a very amused expression on his face. Watching his body move in the water was hypnotic. He was surely toying with her, but why?

She spun around and paced like a caged animal. "Where's John?" This game was not fun anymore.

"He's inside," he said nonchalantly.

She balled her hands into fists and pressed her lips into a tight line. They'd strung her along for long enough. "I'm going to go find him. I have a few words," she said in a huff.

"Your impatience is very sexy," he said right before she pulled the sliding door open.

Hmmmm. Well. That was something, she guessed. She flung herself around to face him. "Oh?"

"Yes, your desire and passion are showing in it." Now he was mocking her too? Her lust was not a toy!

She flipped around back to face the house.

"Laney," he called in a commanding voice that piqued the interest of her clit.

She turned around and watched him climb the steps out of the pool. Each step out of the water showed another delicious six inches of his body. Once he stepped out of the water at the crotch level, she sighed, melting at the sight of his fully engorged penis through his wet clingy suit.

It looked ornately magnificent.

"Oh, my fucking fuck. Holy fuck. Just. Wow. Look at you." She strolled towards him as if in a trance. She'd never seen such a beauty of a cock encased in wet fabric in all her life. His eyes called to her mind, and his cock screamed for her pussy. She was instantly putty in his hands. Whatever he wanted, he'd get. He looked so handsome and sexy. She wanted to tackle him to the ground and strip him naked. She craved to give him her whole self to play with for hours and hours until she was as spent as if she'd run a marathon.

Even though she'd just been fuming in anger like a smokestack, she couldn't stop herself from striding up to him and placing her hands on his chest. Her eyes connected with the lust in his before both of their eyes roamed each other's bodies. Her line of sight fell to his middle, and she couldn't stop staring at his big man meat. It was announcing itself like a siren.

And like a flash of lightning, they collided. Their mouths opened as if on a trigger and they kissed deeply. The electricity between them could have lit up the sun.

He roamed her body with his big strong hands as she felt up his wet firm flesh, ending with a strong squeeze of his fattened manhood.

"Oh, I want you so bad, Anderson. Please," she pleaded as he consumed her mouth in a kiss again. "Need you."

"I'm going to fuck you until you can't even stand." He palmed her body roughly as he pressed himself against her small frame.

She started to drop to her knees, but he stopped her and scooped her up into his arms. They didn't stop kissing as he carried her towards the house. She hadn't expected their fucking would take place in the house on such a nice summer evening, but she no longer cared where it happened, she just wanted him mauling her into a multitude of orgasms. She wanted him using her body to climax as much as he would be making her body explode into too many O's to count.

The sliding door opened as they approached it, and Laney spied John holding a cigar. What the hell? He never smoked inside the house. He still had on the robe, but his legs were now bare beneath. He wore a smug expression on his face that also looked amused. He didn't say a thing as they entered the house. He shut the door and walked across the room to sit in the easy chair near the bar.

Anderson had her full attention now, but John's actions rang in the back of her mind as odd. What was her amazing husband up to? It all just didn't fit together and was unlike his usual behavior on sex dates. But then again, he also usually wasn't openly visible when she got fucked. At least not at first. However, this was a different scenario she suddenly realized. This was a second sex date with Anderson, so, this was actually new ground in their hotwife life. It hadn't been long enough or orchestrated in this way as of yet. The newness was super exciting.

She relaxed. Maybe that was it and she needed to just be present in the moment and get the fuck out of her head because it was interfering with her passion. She had buttloads of passion for Anderson, there was zero question of that.

Anderson kissed down her neck, while still holding her in his arms like a baby. She leaned her head back to give him full access to her neck.

He bit her delicate flesh and she squealed.

John chuckled his appreciation but remained silent.

She tried to squirm away from him making a mark on her neck but she couldn't.

He bit her again. "Mine," he said in a firm voice.

He was marking her as his, right in John's presence. But John had delegated this fucking to Anderson, so she decided that made sense and she fully rolled into the acceptance of it. It felt unexpected to have him stake a claim over her like John often did, but then that was also very exciting and arousing. She'd be a claimed whore to two men. That thought thrilled her.

"Yes," she muttered in a soft cooing tone. "Yours," she said in agreement. "Do me."

Her command was her permission, even though he already had her consent. She liked giving it again. It was empowering, and declared that she decided what dicks got to enter her sacred body.

"Oh, I'll do you alright," he said with a growl.

His manly sounds, partnered with the memories of how he fucked her last time, had a monumental effect on her desire and it crescendo-ed like dynamite.

"Yes, fuck me. I'm yours to consume. Please," she pleaded.

"Nice, Anderson. Very well done. Now fuck her like the beast you are. Fuck her hard. Fuck her good. Make her scream. Be merciless."

Now this was more like it. She shed all the impatience of earlier and leaned into the impending mountains of pleasure she was sure to be gifted from both of the men. Her desire swirled about her brain and then slipped out of her pores to dance with Anderson's. He'd be pile-driving himself into her in no time, of that she was assured.

He set her to stand on the floor and took a seat in front of her on the couch. He grabbed her and undressed her in a flash, her dress flung across the room like a vile unwanted piece of trash.

"Gimme those tits," he demanded as he pulled her to him.

Him beneath her in this way was intriguing. He was usually towering over her, dominating her in a mount stance. He roughly grasped her back as he devoured her right nipple. He twisted the left as he ate her tit.

She squealed at his aggressive consumption of her nipples, her head falling back.

"Yessss," John hissed.

Laney felt her body go slack, and Anderson's hold of her strengthened. She didn't think she'd fall with his grip on her, but without it, she knew she'd crumple. He alternated sucking and pinching, twisting, each of her nipples, taking significant time on each before popping to the other. This tit-sucking show went on for longer than Laney had expected, and her nips began to feel raw.

She glanced back at John, and he was stroking his thickened cock with a lecherous look of pleasure plastered on his face. His eyes rolled back as he pumped his cock.

Anderson garnered her attention again as he kissed down her torso. He pulled her mound lips into his mouth, each getting a decent amount of sucking before he slipped the tip of his tongue into her cleft to unearth her bean.

Laney's clitoris was swollen and sensitive and she moaned to let them both know how aroused and ready to be fucked she was. Making the sounds freely always opened her up for more desired sensations.

"Please, more, I need your cock fucking me, Anderson."

He had his own agenda. Or perhaps, it was more John's agenda, because he said, "If she's wet enough, do it now."

The command did something to Laney. It made it solid that she was their toy in this whole production, and she loved it. She wanted John telling her what to do, and she wanted Anderson to do what John wanted to. He was the director of this fuck scene, and him giving orders in a robe with a cigar felt like he was the godfather of it all. This was his show. Why had she let her impatience rule out by the pool? She should have known John's domination was behind it all. She didn't need to question it, and she shouldn't. Her job was to enjoy, and to be enjoyed.

She let Anderson sway her body to his manipulations as he savored her. Being manhandled in this rough manner aroused Laney, and she felt comfort being able to see John this time. She had zero fears as Anderson began to pump his fat fingers along her slit. She didn't think she could stand much longer. She felt like a cooked spaghetti noodle.

He started to finger fuck her at an ever-increasing speed, running his wide thumb along her clit as well. This move stimulated her clit and G spot at once and she raged towards a climax. As she approached her arousal's peak, he pulled his hand away and spun her around to face John, then bent her over.

"Grab your knees," Anderson stated gruffly.

There was no arguing with that tone, and it swelled her clitoral complex further.

John smiled at her bewildered expression as Anderson smacked her ass from behind.

"Again," John commanded.

Anderson's spanks were brutal, but short, being only two.

"Who's in charge, Laney?" John demanded.

"You are Daddy," Laney said in a weak breathy voice.

"That's right." He cleared his throat as he released his cock and sat up straight. "And who decides how Anderson's going to fuck you?"

She moaned as Anderson rubbed her labia lips and mashed his fingers all around her vulva. She mustered the will to stand but was grateful for the support of his hand on her belly.

"You do," she whispered with difficulty.

"Who?" he asked sternly.

"You, Daddy."

"That's right. Good girl."

Anderson handled her pussy roughly, just like she liked, and with his fingers of this other hand pressing her flesh, controlling the angle and position of her body, she was even more turned on. She could come any time.

"Don't you come yet, Laney," John directed in the voice that meant to her he was fully in charge, and this was his decision. Anderson might be fucking her, but John owned her pussy. But only because she'd given it to him. As she'd learned, the sub chooses her Dom, not the other way around.

She was conditioned to John doing orgasm control on her while he fucked her, not while someone else did. But she found it quite delicious that he was going to give her permission when she could come while Anderson nailed her too. She struggled to stop the climax and felt a twitch of it starting on its own, but she garnered her resolve and controlled it. She'd obediently wait for his command, cause it was just that fulfilling.

"Now fuck her, Anderson. Fuck her hard, doggy. Be relentless. If she falls, she falls. Just keep fucking her into the floor."

Even though she wanted all that, to hear John say it was shocking. Her anticipation of Anderson doing just that raged her into the mode of a mindless fuck doll, waiting and riding the edge for her turn to blast free into orgasmic delights. It wasn't a question of if anymore, but when.

If that wasn't enough to turn her on, John stood up and started taking pics with his phone from all angles as Anderson pressed his glorious vein-popping cock inside her wet thickened hole.

She yelled out as his full shaft barged in, but it went in quick with how slippery her love cave was. It was so extraordinarily satiating to finally have him inside her that she groaned out her appreciation. Him finally slamming into her felt like her achievement.

As Anderson began to pound himself into her gruffly, her body bouncing from all the impacts, John cheered them on with grunts.

She was sure he was not videoing because she heard cock stroking sounds as he said, "Yes, just like that. Fuck her, my man. Fuck her good and hard. Get her ready for me. I want her a cum soaked wrecked wench, a floppy and righteously fucked hormone-soaked whore. Make her useless. Senseless. Used." He growled. "Mine."

All the dirty talk ticked up Laney's enjoyment and she sped towards a climax she knew she wasn't going to be able to stop, which was always the best feeling. John would have to punish her if he didn't want her to come yet because she felt the birthing of a titanic monster orgasm that her body would have no way of edging. It was coming for her like a cruise ship plowing uncontrollably into a shore, no brakes possible on this planet could stop its force. She was a goner.

She felt the wave take her. "Please, Daddy ..." She gasped as if her life depended on it. "Please."

Her begging worked because, to her relief and satiation, John said, "Come, Laney, and come hard. Now. Come for your Daddy. Gimme. Give your Daddy what he wants."

The orgasm was unleashed as Anderson brutally penetrated her sacred female pouch on repeat like a brainless piston. Her body unlatched, curled as she fell to the carpet, her body twisting in the sweet agony of a ginormous climax. She grunted and squeaked out sounds she couldn't stop as her body quaked through all the involuntary vaginal contractions. It was a slick downhill coast in the most delicious fashion. Her eyes fluttered closed as her face rubbed the carpet because Anderson didn't stop fucking her just because she had become a limp lifeless sack of flesh. On the contrary, he barraged her with so many hard thrusts, grunting and groaning his way to his own massive climax.

This was quite effective. She came again with as much force as the first time and felt sleepy, floaty, as if on a different plane of existence. It was a dream, an altered state of reality, as she came a third time to his continued poundings of her pussy.

In her haze, Anderson seemed ready to blast his seed inside her, but John said, "Pull out for a second. It's time."

Chapter 4

Laney froze, even though she was motionless already, her brain stalled. Time for what? Laney couldn't imagine much more than what had just occurred. Her brain was set to a thought-deprived cum-drunk space and she couldn't imagine how she'd feel if she came again. She might go unconscious with another full-body orgasm like the ones she's just sufferingly enjoyed. They were so pleasurable, but almost an enduring of some unnamable heavy bliss. But she'd never turn down the experience to be rolled through another one if they decided to push her there. The exhilaration she currently felt could not be topped by anything on the planet.

She tipped over when Anderson left her. A waif of a former woman in control, she felt used, pleasured, and spoiled. It couldn't possibly get better than this. She had to admit she had loved John being present and visible to her while she had gotten fucked by Anderson. It was a new level of excitement and control, compared to when he had been hidden. It was more blatant control on John's part, in her face, and Laney loved it. Him looking into her eyes during had been like him ordering her to take what Anderson shoved up her pussy on repeat. She savored the glorious image.

John stood up and his cock swung. She assumed he was ready to fuck her now. Maybe he was going to do it in front of Anderson again. She'd liked that last time in the backyard. A repeat of that would be very welcome to her.

John walked towards her and, when she made eye contact, her excitement soared. She saw the full Dom mode was blazing in his eyes. She knew the look well. He was going to fuck her rough and skin-smacking relentlessly. It sent a surge through her puffy genitals. She was ready and wanted it from him. She adored when he burned bright and out of control in his most dominant phase. He commanded her like no one had ever in the world, and she desired to give herself fully to him. She knew she'd openly submit to him, giving of herself like a gift for him to unwrap, toy with, pleasure, mount, fuck, use, drain. And he'd give her back to herself in full, orgasm drenched and fully and delightfully spent. She was his, but she was her own at once.

He lined up behind her next to Anderson and her heart jumped off a cliff and sent adrenaline to all her extremities like bolts of lightning. It was going to happen. In a flash like something breaking, she was both terrified and elated.

John gripped her hips firmly and aggressively flipped her to her back. He spread her legs swiftly as he made more direct eye contact with her. His gaze was confident and commandeering. The way he handled her body, anyone watching would know he owned her. Not like a possession, never like that, but as her sexual leader, her generous caretaking man, her brilliant champion of a lover, her all-encompassing director of orgasmic pleasure.

And he was her dream.

She lay flaccid and wanton as they lined themselves up between her thighs. Her pussy lips felt puffy and warm, even verging on hot. The throbbing was exhausting, but she felt so coated in goodness that she didn't want it all to not happen. She was ready for it.

"Are you ready for two cocks in your whore of a cunt, babe?" John's voice was garbled and gruff.

She nodded and meekly, yet with full confidence reigning inside her, she adamantly said, "Yes."

They both pressed their cock heads at her slit, one on top of the other. Their bodies were slightly askew so they'd have the room to get their erections in her.

She gasped as John penetrated her lips first.

"Yes, I want you both to fuck me." She sounded so needy, which was in contrast to how satiated she felt.

With John inside her, Anderson pushed his cockhead into her too.

Pain bled to her every cell in her pubic area and she cried out. She hadn't expected this, but told herself to breathe and relax.

"Oh my ..." she spewed. "Fuck!"

Her pussy strained to take the double cock load as they both thrust into her. Then, much to her relief, it happened. Once her cunt walls accepted them inside her, the luxurious joyride started. The double pump, the rub in multiple spots of her womanhood inside and out, the thought of their cocks rubbing together inside her, launched her straight on full blast towards the climax like the trajectory of a shot bullet. She screamed as she lost all control of her body and the contractions owned her as they pulsed out. They were so strong, she jerked involuntarily, her head tilted, her body curled up making her shoulders leave the ground, and she couldn't say it but the word 'fuck' blasted her brain like a bomb going off.

John came first with a roar, and Anderson grunted his out next.

It was a short, but very intense and hot experience, and immediately Laney looked forward to the next time they doubly vaginally fuck her. This wouldn't be near enough of it.

She'd asked for this, the DV, and John had delivered, once again proving to her that he made her his priority, and her pleasure the topmost of their sexual play. This was also how Laney yearned in perfect jubilation to give herself fully to her man. She couldn't ever imagine giving herself to anyone other than John, it literally was not possible. She'd chosen him, and that was it. No wiggle room, so shifting power to Anderson, other than what John deemed him.

"Oh, my fucking gawd," Laney said as she panted, the sensations reverberating around her body overwhelming her to the point she was motionless.

Both men crashed on either side of her, panting heavily as well.

"Unbelievable," Anderson muttered, his voice revealing his shock.

"Fucking amazing, kickass, and out of this world," John said with a happy and satiated tone.

"No shit," Laney said. Forming long sentences was just not in her wheelhouse at the moment. She felt like a survivor who'd mastered a challenge, and it felt like a decree.

They laid out flat on the carpet panting together as they all floated back down off the gargantuan high.

"You guys just blew all my fantasies out of the water. I seriously can't thank you enough for choosing me for this. I'm honored to be here." Anderson's tone was reverent and respectful. "I fucking loved it," he said with clear, and delicious, enjoyment. "That was an untoppable experience."

"Yes, it was, and she deserved it."

Laney felt pampered by all they'd done to her, and by what they had said. "Thank you, John. Thank you, Anderson." It was only right to give them each their own 'thank you'.

John sat up, his cock now at a semi. "I think we all need a drink and perhaps something sweet. What do you both think?"

"I'm in," Anderson stated as he stood up.

"I'm afraid my body feels like Jell-O." Her voice quivered a bit and a shiver torqued through her body. She was gifted a late aftershock in her pussy as she smiled. "Aftershocks."

John grinned. "I love your aftershocks. Especially when I'm still inside you."

He scooped her up and gently laid her on the couch. "You two wait here, I'll be right back." John changed the music to something calming and disappeared up the stairs.

"Anderson, oh wow, that was incredible, really. I've never been fucked so amazingly and thoroughly before."

He raised an eyebrow. "It wasn't too rough for you? I was afraid it may have been too much for you."

"Oh, hell no, fuck no. And I'd tell you if it was." She smiled at him as he got settled on the other end of the couch. "That was not just mind-blowing, but life-altering." She rolled her head against the soft couch as she hugged the pillow John had placed over her breasts. "Just fucking incredible, I don't even have the right words."

"Good. Because that's about where I'm at too. And I know this is all because of you two, not because of me. I'm just the brute force with the cock. This is all you guys."

"No. That's not true. If you weren't how you are, you wouldn't fit with us. So, you play an integral and important part too." She squeezed the pillow. "We are unique, and none of this would happen without all of us being the people we are."

He nodded with deliberation, as if he really understood what she meant. "Yeah, I suppose you're right. I'm not just the cock." He grinned a sexy yet humble grin.

"Never just a cock, but what an amazing cock you do have!" she exclaimed. "Your cock couldn't ever fit the phrase 'just a cock.'"

He looked pleased and it cradled her even more.

They talked about his work for a few minutes while they waited for John to return. Laney didn't mind the alone time to chat with Anderson because it helped her feel even more in line with him. She really did enjoy his company, not just how raucously he fucked her.

"Happy hour is served." John appeared with a tray.

He had brought three cocktails, some chocolates, the angel food cake, whipped cream, and fruit.

"Wow, this looks incredible!" Laney was certainly famished.

She sipped her drink as she grabbed for a piece of dark chocolate. She sighed happily as she chewed. "Yummy."

"So," John said as he patted her thigh from where he was seated between her and Anderson. "What was it like? You seemed at first that you didn't like it. Did it hurt?"

She sighed. "Yes. It did. But once I relaxed and my body adjusted to both of you, it turned into pure fucking bliss." She grinned big at him. "I absolutely loved it and want to do it again."

John sighed a big sigh of relief. "Good. I was a bit concerned. To be honest, I almost halted the whole thing until I saw your face change to pleasure."

"Yeah, I felt that, too," Anderson stated.

"It was touch and go for about a minute and a half, and I almost said the safe word."

John nodded while he chewed. "And me being present while he fucked you? How was that for your arousal and enjoyment?"

She nodded profusely as she finished chewing another chocolate. "It was stellar. I really loved you in the room. We need to do that more often. And I loved how you directed us. It really ticked off my sub checklist of what turns me on."

"I enjoyed it too, babe. I'm definitely in for more of that."

"Again, I have to thank you two."

"Stop!" Laney shrieked. "Anderson, you are fully wanted and a part of this. Stop acting like a guest."

He released a curt laugh. "Ah, ok. I get it, Laney. It feels really good. Thanks."

"Good. You were the man railing her like that. You sent her through so many orgasms. I should be thanking you for giving my lovely, deserving wife so much pleasure. You helped me satisfy her immensely today."

"Well, it was my pleasure. I got as much as I gave."

They continued to enjoy the night, fully clothed, and sipping beverages on the patio. Once darkness fell, Anderson graciously took his leave, and to

Laney's protests, thanked the both of them again. He left with a wave before exiting the side gate door.

"Epic. And I love you. And epic." She paused and shook her head. "John you're amazing. Just when I think you can't outdo yourself, you do. Thank you, the love of my life."

"Focusing on you just accelerates my inner Dom. This happens because of you. You do this to me."

She leaned over the edge of the table and pursed her lips. They kissed.

"And you do this to me."

"Love you, babe. Guess we should make our way to bed."

She sighed and rose from her chair. "Yep, I'm very sleepy. I could have fallen asleep on the floor after you two fucked me like that."

"I know, I had half of a mind to let you, too."

"Never stop this," she pleaded with love pooled in her eyes.

"Never will."

"Pushing the limits with you is ecstasy." She hip-checked him with a playful expression.

He pulled her into a hug beneath the star-packed night sky.

"Anything with you is. I'm gonna say it again, I'm the luckiest man on Earth."

"Same. Only not a man," she said with a laugh.

"Let's get to bed. I'm an old man and I need my rest."

She giggled at him. "I'm ready for rest myself. You do tend to break our records to beat my pussy into the most orgasms I've ever had in one day."

"Oh, yeah? I hadn't thought of that."

"Yup, I think today was the top."

"Well, that gives me the best next challenge, then."

They collected their empty glasses, plates, and used napkins and made their way into the house, satisfied and stoked for the next sexual adventure.

Servicing the Handy Man,
A Leisurely Working Retiree

Book 4

Chapter 1

Laney pulled up her bikini bottoms and smiled, her heart still pounding violently, like she'd just run for her life. She swiveled just in time to see John turn and wave to her through the sliding glass door with a giant grin plastered across his handsome face. They had just had the best sex ever, so she was glowing. He had meandered out to the pool on a work break and taken her in a rush of passion, bent over the garden table under the beating of the afternoon's strongest sunrays. The earthy smell of her little gardening shovel had made for a primal experience, the natural aroma wafting into her nostrils from inches away as John had pressed her down to the rough surface of the tall table to fuck her from behind. She had just used the shovel to dig out a huge, stubborn weed in the garden before he had come out.

She glanced at her hands and chuckled at how they were still coated in black earth. She sauntered over to the garden hose and turned the metal knob lefty loosey so she could blast the dirt off her skin with the frigid blast of water. The water felt nice in the heat, cooling her a bit. Now she'd need a dip in the pool to cool down the rest of her body. After a hot sex session under the blazing August sun, she needed that to wash off the heat from the sun and the encounter with John.

Marvin was coming today to work on putting up some shelves she wanted added to their bedroom closet. Marvin had become their go-to for handyman jobs around the house. Not that John couldn't do these things, but he was just so busy with work that these extra tasks were adding stress. Plus, they took time away from Laney. John wanted Laney to have what she wanted, but with his incessant work schedule he was finding it a challenge to keep up with her home improvements. So Marvin had become their go-to solution.

Laney bit her lip. Marvin was a very sexy older man of sixty-six, almost sixty-seven, he had told her with a twinkle in his eyes the last time he had been at the house. He had a head of white hair with remnants of dark still present at some of the ends. He had told her with amusement that he was almost full grown now that he'd gotten nearly a full head of white. Retirement had seemed to be sitting well with Marvin because he always appeared to be in a very good mood.

He held a comforting Daddy-like persona, one that blared he was capable of fixing anything, but also very capable of taking care of a woman. He was single, as far as she knew, and was enjoying life as an unattached man, or so he claimed. He seemed happy every time he came to the house. It was a happiness that seemed to come from his core, not some narcissistic phony mask, like plastic that he'd removed when not in front of others, or when not getting his way. His genuineness also shone out of him as bright as the boldest sunshine in how he always interacted with her. He was mega hot, and Laney had told John she found him sexy, so she had a glimmer of hope that someday something might happen.

Laney also knew men got better at pleasing a woman as they aged, so she figured Marvin would likely be a fantastic lover, and she yearned to taste his version of sex.

Her loins stirred as she imagined him approaching her and giving her oral, his scalp of white hair bobbing between her thighs. Her fingers meandered to her outer lower lips through her bikini bottoms. Even though John had just made her come four times as he railed her, she was ready for more. She hoped John had spoken with Marvin already and that he'd seduce her with John's permission. It would most definitely be delicious. But John hadn't indicated anything about it. She both loathed and loved his surprises, but only because she was impatient and horny. She just wanted it to happen, and soon.

She slipped into the refreshing pool water and sighed as the water snatched the heat from her body. Instantly, she hated the bikini hindering the flow of the water along her flesh, so she removed it and tossed it to her lounge chair.

"Woohoo! I made it," she cheered as the bottoms hit the chaise just as she heard the gate lock latch click.

Marvin strode into the backyard wearing a pair of loose gray lounge shorts and a lime green t-shirt. She loved all the colors he wore; he wasn't afraid to don any color, which always made him look like he was a fun guy to be around. Which, so far, had proved to be right, only Laney hadn't been around him much other than for the business of getting the little jobs done around the house.

She glanced down and snickered. How was she to know Marvin would stroll into her backyard at this moment? He usually went to the front door.

"Oh, hey, Laney, how are you?" His eyes were warm, and his expression was friendly. "John told me to come on back. He wants me to fix your busted garden box, too."

Laney had forgotten about the broken box, but she felt warm inside knowing John hadn't. "Oh, very nice. Yeah, it's the one with the tomato plants in the right back corner of the garden."

Laney watched with scrumptious relish as Marvin's gaze went from her to the bikini bottoms on the chair, and back to her.

His grin widened, and he released a chuckle. "Perfect day for a skinny dip." He pointed at the sun. "Nice and hot. Hope you've fully sun screened."

She loved that he was staring at her naked body in the pool and she wished her top was off too. "Yes, I did, and, yes, it feels incredible." She swam about, allowing the water to slide along her pussy lips and ass crack. "It's a slice of heaven to be able to do this in the privacy of my backyard anytime I want."

He raised his eyebrows. "Indeed. You are very lucky." He paused as a smirk grew. "And so is John."

She wanted Marvin to get lucky too and opened her mouth to speak, but John emerged from the basement.

"Hey, Marvin, and one more thing, could you fix Laney's garden table? It's a little rocky, one of the legs is a bit loose, I think."

John gave Laney a knowing glance. He had made the table ricketier by fucking her like a beast, ramming his big swollen cock into her on repeat.

She returned the look. "Oh, yeah. It's gotten a bit more unstable recently." She stifled a laugh while letting her lewd memories flood her face.

John mirrored her appreciation, and they held each other's gazes. "Darn thing isn't as sturdy as it used to be, getting used often the way it does."

Laney laughed, loving John talking about their fuck session to Marvin without actually saying it.

"Sure thing, boss, you got it," Marvin said with a salute and a big, happy grin. He clearly liked doing the small jobs. "Keeps me busy, and out of trouble."

Laney wanted Marvin to get into trouble, though, with her. It wouldn't be a John scheme if Lancy knew the full story, but John had this gleam in his eye, and that usually meant glorious things for Laney. Her stomach swirled into a flurry as she let her mind start to imagine what lecherous plan might be lighting that spark in his eyes. She couldn't wait to be in the know.

"Then, if you can move to the bedroom, Laney can go up with you and show you exactly what she wants done." John winked at Laney as he scooped up her bikini bottom and stuffed it in his pocket.

Laney's eyes popped out of her head when he also snatched her towel, and then started to head inside.

Whoa! What was this?

He waved the towel in the air like a flag as Laney watched, open-jawed, as he went inside.

Holy fuck. This was obviously intentional. But was Marvin in on it? Or was she supposed to seduce Marvin in the bedroom? Or was John just signaling his permission by this act, and that it was Laney's decision of free will with his blessing on what she'd do with Marvin?

Her libido blossomed as she watched Marvin working. Would he respond well if she just climbed out of the pool naked and asked him to fuck her? Would he be aghast and scamper off, never to grace their house again? Had John briefed Marvin on her being a hotwife or was she going into this seduction cold, and it was all on her?

The unknowns were both terrifying and exciting. She knew Marvin's eyes had roamed her before. A woman can tell when a man finds her attractive, and Marvin most certainly had given her those cues on multiple occasions. Her heart began to race as Marvin glanced her way, and then he did again.

"How did this bust out? It should be good now."

"I don't know, one day it just loosened, and the dirt spilled out, widening it."

He straightened up, still wearing a grin. As he walked out of the garden, she spied a slight bulge in his shorts. She hoped it wasn't a mirage, or just wishful thinking.

"Now to that table." He made his way towards it and memories of hot sex flooded her brain once more.

She imagined Marvin taking her over it, pressing his man meat up her hot, moist cunt like a wet piston on full power. She sighed and shuddered. She was ready to rush him and offer her body to him, but she still wished John had given her a clearer direction. She knew he'd never be mad at her if she fucked

Marvin. That was the goal, to fuck other men. John loved her being a hotwife, and getting pleasure, especially because it made her a wanton, insatiable slut, and he always reaped the fruit of it the most. Well, Laney chuckled to herself, with multiple orgasms possible, she was the one who reaped the most benefit of anyone. John wanted her as cum-drunk as often as possible. He was a wonderful man. She'd learned to climax up to sixty times a day with his help, though she recently heard on a podcast that the female clitoris is wired to circuit 286 times a day. Talk about ensuring the continuation of the species! That was a damn solid plan. So, being at sixty for her O achievements, she had lots of room to improve.

Marvin rocked the table and it moved slightly. "Yup. Just one leg coming loose. I'll tighten it up for you." He knelt down and looked under the table again, then stood and flipped it over. He placed it on the little drink table next to the Adirondack chairs around the bonfire pit. "Easy as pie."

Within a few minutes, he had the table back upright and was showing Laney it no longer rocked. For now, she snickered.

She knew John might quickly unfix Marvin's handiwork, but that was part of the naughty fun, anyway. And they paid Marvin quite well for his handyman work. It was a win-win all around.

"Okay, on to the next task." His eyes drifted to Laney and his expression grew suggestive, almost leery.

She shivered in excitement as she swam to the stairs, ready and lusting to emerge from the water half-naked and randy like a wet, sex-hungry goddess. On a last-minute whim, she untied and slipped off her top and released it in the pool.

Marvin held her direct gaze as she ascended the stairs. Her breasts bounced slightly as she emerged from the water, then with more swing once they hit full air.

"I'll show you to the bedroom," she said in an alluring voice. She intended to stroll right past John, and hopefully she'd glean a bit more info from his reaction as she walked past him naked, with Marvin in tow. "Right this way."

Laney knew Marvin already knew where their bedroom was, so this told her that John wanted her to do something. He'd done so many jobs that he'd been in every room of the house by this point, and more than once. But to Laney, the thought of guiding him through the house as he watched her bare ass tick-tock in front of him was a seduction she most certainly wanted a part of.

Chapter 2

She slid open the sliding door to a chilling blast of air conditioning, which hardened her nipples to stiff peaks. That, combined with her pussy lips flaring open with her extreme horniness and readiness for cock as she felt Marvin's presence behind her, was almost too much to bear already. She needed more, and she needed it now.

She stopped when she caught John's gaze. He was on a call and gave her a nod, but his expression was all business, with nothing indicating any sort of instructions at all.

With her abrupt stop, Marvin bumped into her butt cheeks.

"Oh," she exclaimed, but then grinned salaciously as she felt his erection when his body met hers.

"Oh, my dear, I'm so very sorry, I wasn't paying attention, clearly." Marvin's voice was tender and apologetic.

She glanced back at him with a knowing, seductive look. "Oh, it was my pleasure."

His facial expression turned flirty. "Oh, on the contrary, I think it was mine."

Well, that wasn't nothing, and Marvin clearly knew John was in earshot.

She started for the stairs when John didn't return her look. So she was on her own. That was just fine. Whether John had prepped Marvin or not, the fun would be in finding out, and then acting on it.

She climbed the stairs, loving the fact that Marvin was right on her heels, watching her naked ass. She was getting hotter by the second, knowing his eyes must be on her bare goose-pimpled wet flesh. "It's just this way."

Laney had always loved walking around naked in the house, even when she hadn't been this open sexually. There was just something so sensual about it, which piqued her desire even higher as she led Marvin to her and John's master suite. The excitement of the unknown thrilled her and she felt her lower lips slide across each other very easily as she moved. She was quite wet, and not just from the pool water.

She fought the urge to touch Marvin as they entered the closet. What she really wanted was to grab him and run her hand over that mound at his crotch and give it a nice firm squeeze, hoping that would entice him to put his hands on her.

"Well," she said, realizing she was flat-out panting, and it wasn't from climbing all the stairs. She was way too in shape for that to be a thing. "I want these shelves to replace the ones that are there, and then add these other two in the open space." She waved her hands around to further indicate to him what she wanted.

"Okay, that's easy. It won't take me long at all." He gave her a confident look. "I'm quite experienced. I know exactly what to do to get you what you want."

It didn't feel like he was talking about shelves, and the fire in his eyes confirmed it. "Oh, really now," she said with desire swarming in her tone. "Now that I'd really love to ... experience." She gave him intense fuck me eyes, and feeling bold, she asked, "Did John talk with you?"

"Yes," he whispered. "He said you get whatever you want, and that I can help." He raised an eyebrow above his lusty, hungry eyes. "And I very, very, very, very much want to help you, Laney."

Electric jolts pierced her body and then heated her up further as his words sunk into her cum-hungry brain. Yes! "Wow. That sounds very intriguing indeed."

"Just say the word, and it's yours." His voice was low, patient, and full of desire, and that was intoxicating to her.

He was looking for clear permission, and she loved that. It was sexy to give her full consent, especially when she also knew John had given his. The impending pleasure she was about to receive filled her body full of explosive excitement. She might burst, and he hadn't even touched her yet.

"Yes, please, I'd love to have sex with you." For some reason, him being older made her feel like she shouldn't use vulgar words. Maybe it was his refined presence, his gentlemanly manner, his distinguished maturity, but she felt the need to be a little more proper, though she rather hoped they'd get raunchy as fuck. Imagining him spewing dirty talk made her clit thicken.

He smiled the most delicious smile and a proud expression settled upon his face. "Good girl," he said in an approving tone that didn't feel a bit condescending to Laney at all, mostly because she craved that phrase like the air itself.

She smiled back, feeling her inner sweetheart bloom. "Yes," she repeated, waiting anxiously to experience his next move.

"May I kiss you?" he asked with a simple shifting of his eyes down and up her body.

She nodded, feeling herself slip into his fatherly-like leading guidance. Her submissive bone was getting tweaked pretty aggressively deep inside her. He had a Dom look in his eyes similar to what John often sported, only it was more pronounced, knowing, and likely from more years of sex. Being ravaged by the strong, full-body thrusts of Anderson was always intoxicating, but Marvin was proving to be a whole different sexual animal entirely. Her lust seethed into a fierce ball of fire.

He caressed her arms and her face, smoothing and running his fingers through her hair gently, while she raged silently and impatiently inside to feel his tongue entering her. She opened her mouth with an insistent, bratty sentence about to emerge when he pressed his finger to her lips.

"Shhhh. I want to enjoy your supple flesh for a few moments right now. Cradle your senses first."

Oh, she felt lulled alright, but also very ready to be railed by him like a racquet smacking a tennis ball on repeat.

"Taking my time to savor a woman's beauty, your beauty, Laney, is what I treasure." He continued to finger and caress her body, lightly touching her stomach, her hips, then sliding his hands ever so lightly over her bottom. His apparent control of his passion was intoxicating.

She gasped as he snugged a finger like a feather along her ass crack.

His words scooped her mind up, sending her spirit soaring. Feeling floaty, but grounded by lust, she knew she'd be his instrument for both their pleasures, but at his pace. She wanted him to be in charge, just as John always was in the bedroom. Being led through sexual bliss was such a turn-on, and she had an inkling Marvin was even more masterful than John at this. She had hopes, anyway. Experience and maturity were promising to be a turn-on with this silver fox.

His soft touches continued as his eyes shone softly, which hinted at swollen controlled lust scrumptiously laden inside, just waiting patiently for the explosive satiation to come.

What wonderful bliss this was! She was so aroused she felt pulled into a dream, yet full of a growing desire to feel the press of his body to hers. It was so simple, so sensuous, and so calm, yet ripe with sexual elation. She soaked up the suggestive intent in his eyes, lulled by his magic, and fell against him as he pulled her body to his.

His mouth on her flesh was soft and wet, gentle and indulgent, seeming both for him and for her. His kisses spoke of burning yet patient passion, having a handle on lust to a level she had not yet been gifted the presence of. He kissed the tops of her breasts, slathering his tongue slowly along as if he were savoring a decadent meal. His soft moans of appreciation commandeered her attention as she acquiesced to his lead, happily giving in to his slower, more sensual pace. She certainly was not used to being cherished so meticulously in this manner, and it was both shocking and lovely at once. John was always more of a rush of brutish and blazing passion than the lingerer Marvin was proving to be. Not that he didn't take time to please her relentlessly, but this was somehow different. She was enjoying the slow burn with Marvin.

He caressed her right nipple with his fingers, his touch so light and airy, and sufficiently arousing on a new level. He took her tightened tit between his lips, carefully nibbling around its mound as he firmly supported her back with both hands. He flicked her nipple with the tip of his tongue before suckling the nub, then the full areola. He increased his consumption of her full nipple, drawing it to the back of his throat. He stroked her nipple with his undulating tongue as he sucked.

She let her head fall back and released a series of moans as he loved up her nipple. When he pressed his teeth to her flesh, she wanted to scream. She was so ready to be fucked, but his calm sensuality held her at bay. She had to admit, she was gleefully giving in to the brand of his seduction.

He dined on her nipple some more before giving her other one similar treatment. Her arousal hung just below, begging for his cock up her though, but she decided she'd follow his lead and lean into the slow foreplay. Her rage was there, though, like a flurry of fire under a grate, but with his deliberate display of cherishing affection, she could quiet it, for the moment at least.

It struck her that it might be a version of obeying.

He continued to suckle along her skin as she fed her fingers into his shock of lush, white hair. His head bobbed and she relished his tit sucking as she finger-combed his short locks. With a slow rise like this, Laney knew she'd come quick and often when they finally got to the fucking.

He licked up her torso, from her pussy mound to her neck before opening his mouth to kiss her slowly and on the surface at first, then gradually sending his tongue ever deeper. The man knew how to kiss, which made Laney weak in the knees.

At her falter, he leaned his tall frame down to scoop her up like a baby. "I'm not your Dom. A girl can only have one Dom, but John said we can role-play it, if you want, baby." His face was soft and understanding. "It will be only at your will and your permission, though."

There she had it. They had discussed him fucking her. Not that she had doubted it, but it felt comforting and affirming to hear it from Marvin's lips. She relaxed even further in this absolute indication of permission from John. John sure liked to keep her guessing, which was part of the fun and the game of it.

She grinned with deepening relish. "Yes, I know what you mean. A girl can only have one Daddy." She'd chosen John as hers and no one else could fill his shoes. She could sense Marvin was a Dom, though. She had seen all the signs that hinted at it in how he treated her, respected her, not that such things were truly enough for full proof, but the impression of dominance was very evident. He also was placing her pleasure as a priority, while his actions spoke of nurturing indulgence, sure signs of a Daddy Dom. She wondered instantly if he had a sub and if they were in an open relationship with him, engaging with her like this.

"I can see your wheels turning, Laney," he said calmly. "But that's a story for later."

She had no choice but to accept his dictation on this. But he was lulling her into his putty quite sufficiently, so she didn't mind waiting at all.

He laid her on the bed and stroked her full body slowly and lovingly, like he was making a map of her body inside his brain. The slow deliberation he was taking was the ultimate seduction for Laney. She'd never been with a man this much older than her before, and it excited her. She loved the whole Daddy

Dom image, the mature man who knew what he was doing in bed, the careful and intentional lover. A masculine leader in the bedroom was her ultimate kink. It made her weak in the knees.

She instantly wondered if calling him 'Daddy' was an okay thing. She felt like saying it, but John was her Daddy. Maybe she could just avoid calling him anything, or perhaps she could say 'Sir'. Or 'Dad', but that felt weird because that's what she called her dad. She mulled it over in her head as he cupped, stroked, caressed, and kissed her from head to toe.

He stood up and began to remove his clothes. Before climbing back on the bed, while holding her gaze intently, he asked carefully, "Do you desire to be with me, Laney?"

She nodded vehemently. "Yes, very much so, Marvin. Please." She was relieved that calling him 'Marvin' felt right. But she yearned to call him something sexier, raunchier, hotter.

"Do you like rough sex or tender sex?" The look in his eyes told her he already knew.

"Yes," she said confidently, with a sly grin.

"Good girl," he said with obvious approval. "Let's be honest, and we can have some real fun together. Okay?"

Laney's mind wandered as she imagined him in both of those modes. She couldn't wait to experience them both at his hands, and at his cock, and especially at his mercy. He was a very fit, slender, muscular man. When he revealed his cock to her, she was elated. It was thick and solid looking, with the top half a bit lighter in color than the lower half, sort of a two-tone skin pattern. He had all his pubic hair and she wanted to feel it with her cheeks, her hands, and spongy against her flesh. His blue eyes were soft and kind, yet still held a level of intensity that explained it all about him and his demeanor. This was a gift to be with such an epic and experienced man. John had done well to prep him too because he was hitting her hot spots of her neck, her bottom, her breasts, and her face. Now she needed him to lay hands on her clit.

She moaned and writhed against his caresses as he became more aggressive with his touches and grabs. His expression became fiercer as he began to thrust his packed hard-on against her.

"You are so soft, so sexy, Laney. I've always admired you, and lusted for you. I couldn't believe my good fortune when John approached me about being with you." His gaze was turning hungrier by the minute.

Her mind spun, but she was thrilled Marvin was of the same mindset as she and John. When had they talked? What had John said? Her questions died off as the pleasure he was pulling her into grew.

He suckled his way down her body, and she shivered with glee when he settled between her thighs. A knowing grin rested on his face as he paused before dropping to her pussy. He inhaled deeply and licked her closed lips.

"You smell delicious," he whispered into her sealed slit. He slurped up her closed womanhood several more times as she squirmed.

"Please," she pleaded.

"Please, what?"

She sighed as her desire for even the slightest touch from him began to consume her. "Please, more."

She wasn't sure what he was fishing for, but she calmed when he said, "Good girl."

He nudged her pussy lips open with the tip of his tongue. He swirled all along her lips, taking time every twenty seconds to visit and flick her thickening bean. She grasped at the sheets and yelled out when he suctioned his mouth tight over her clit. He pressed two fingers gently and just barely into her wet slit and tickled his other fingers all along her hole and across her lips.

His slow approach was driving her wild, and she wanted to scream and beg for more. He continued to increase his pressure as he inserted more fingers into her molten hole further. He began to pump his fingers into her quickly and forcefully as he aggressively mouthed her clit. It sent her skyrocketing towards her first climax with him. She blissfully blasted off the big O edge with a series of moans, and a yelp, followed by a long silence as her womb instinctively convulsed with contractions. She gasped repeatedly as it settled down. Her panting and whimpers continued, though, because he didn't stop.

She panicked with a screech when he manipulated her overly sensitive clitoral head and she slammed into a triple-peaked orgasm, all the while her body arching, twitching, her heels raised off the bed, her knees bent. Oh, the sounds she was making! If only John could hear.

He proceeded to make her come with his mouth on her aroused female parts like a fragrance to flower, as if they were one, not one existing without the other.

After she'd come so many times that she felt floppy and cum-saturated, he pointed to the window and said and a very stern voice she wouldn't dare question, "Get over to that window, lean your bare tits against it, point your naked ass towards me. I'm going to fuck your pussy from behind for all the world to see."

Chapter 3

She didn't move. Her brain must not be working right because she couldn't fathom how he'd gone from pleasuring her so thoroughly to this commanding persona. She remained frozen, staring at him wide-eyed, but her desire roared.

Marvin grabbed her roughly and pointed at the window.

"Over there, Laney. I want to fuck you against that window for the world to see," he grumbled in a repeat of that succulent phrase, the first flaring of his impatient passion making an appearance in his voice.

She desired to experience his loss of control. The combination of the tender, satisfying oral sex, then the idea of his rough fucking her in an exhibitionistic way was driving Laney wild. Her excitement surged as she scrambled to the window and pressed her big fleshy tits against the glass. It was warm from the sunshine. She pressed her cheek to the window as she saw her neighbor to the right mowing his lawn. Luckily, it was too early in the afternoon for any kids to be off the buses and wandering the streets yet.

He roughly grasped her hips and gave her ass a single hard spank.

She got it. He was in charge. And it was comforting and wanted.

"You have such a beautiful body, Laney. I can't wait to fuck you until you are spent and weak from pleasure. I'm gonna fuck you hard. Really hard."

She had no doubts about that and had been waiting for this moment since they had first embraced, to be about to get his full sexual fury filled her with elation.

He slapped his hard-on against her buttocks, spanking her with it several times. Laney smiled. It was like he was winding up a bat.

He pressed his cockhead at her entrance and gave a slow, penetrating push. His cock easily entered her core, and he ramped up his thrusts to a fast pace without any hesitation. He rocked her body from behind and her tits slid on the window. She pressed her palms flat as he pounded her ever harder from behind. She increased the pressure of her hands against the glass to try to stabilize herself.

He pulled her back and felt up her tits, tugged on her nipples as he chugged himself in and out of her. Then he grabbed her hips hard and fucked her way harder than she had thought an older man could fuck her.

She writhed and moaned, feeling floppy as a blade of long grass in the wind as he railed her beast mode.

"Who's your Daddy?" he demanded between pants.

Laney was silent. She was confused. He had just agreed a girl could only have one dominant, one Daddy. But then, he had also said it was her choice and that John had given them the green light to role-play, just for fun. Her mind careened as she tried to mull over what to do. He was fucking her so commandingly that her brain didn't work quite right.

He slapped her ass and then kept shoving his cock into her. He reached around and pressed her clit and rubbed it.

"Answer me, you whore," he demanded as he drilled her.

She shivered as his dirty talk ramped up her excitement further.

He slapped her right ass cheek again, hard.

Her mind stalled. She couldn't fathom what the right answer was.

He stopped pumping into her and leaned into her ear. "Do what you feel, Laney. Don't think. Just do."

She shuddered as he gripped her body forcefully, imbedding her with his cock balls deep.

He began to pump into her again.

She sighed and moaned as he played with her clit while pounding against her butt. She felt lulled into the sensations of submitting to him and it was lush, luxurious, and it felt right. "Daddy," she whispered meekly, but with full confidence in what she had chosen to call him.

"Good girl. Very good girl." He thrust into her so hard she felt her body might break the glass.

Her orgasm loomed close, and all she could do was succumb. She gasped for more as she opened her eyes and spied some movement in the driveway. What was that? As Marvin rammed himself into her and her bare tits rubbed the window in a fast gyration, she dismissed it. Who the fuck cared when she was getting this royally and graciously fucked?

Marvin took a step back and his cock fell out of Laney's pussy.

Confused, she remained against the window, awaiting his next instruction. She knew better than to move before he gave her a command. She waited with bated breath as he walked away from her. Still, she remained frozen like a good girl, but she felt her impatience swelling. What could Marvin be doing? Looking for a dildo? A clit sucker? Needing to ask John something?

Now that she was alone, her eyes began to wander about the front yard. She wondered who'd seen her body rubbing on the window as Marvin had fucked her. She figured her neighbor mowing the lawn likely had, but he was always peeping at them anyway, so that was nothing new. But who else had seen her being fucked from behind? Surely there must have been someone driving by or out walking their dog. The possibility thrilled her and charged up her lust even higher. She'd love it if her neighbor, Ben, had seen. He was so sexy, and he was on her bucket list to exercise her hotwife bone with and she had shared that with John last week. She could only hope he'd agree and set up the date. He was newly divorced, because his ex-wife had gone off to Florida with her new lover, and she had given him the house. They had planned to live in Florida anyway, but now it was just her. Laney hadn't seen any women over at his house, but the divorce was still pretty fresh, and likely painful. But she'd happily give him her pussy to pound as rebound medicine.

Laney held her breath as she heard footsteps. Maybe John was coming to join? She hoped so. She'd love to be railed by both John and Marvin. Maybe another vaginal DP? Or a good ol' spit roast? A two-man bukkake? Any way they'd form their man-dominated threesome, she was in.

She heard male voices that were faint but got louder as she sensed them approaching her. She strained to hear the other voice, but it was too hushed to make out.

"I've made her come half a dozen times, then fucked her pretty forcefully against the window, but she hasn't come there as far as I can tell." Marvin was giving John the play-by-play, which made her smile.

She adored getting sexually served, plus she secretly loved it when the men would talk about her as if she weren't there. It was like they were creating the experience for her, and in addition, being treated like a sex object sat just right with her desires. She bit her lip, wishing she could see their expressions as they stared at her bare ass with her tits still smashed against the glass for all the world to see.

"Laney, I'm going to put a blindfold on you. I have a surprise for you, but I don't want you to know what it is yet." Marvin had a commanding tone that was so delicious, it made her quiver.

She nodded. "Okay, Daddy." It felt yummy, yet a bit taboo to be calling Marvin 'Daddy' in front of John. She stifled a laugh. It was like Dr. Seuss. But not Thing One and Thing Two, but Daddy One and Daddy Two. She considered calling them that, with John, of course, being number one. It was playtime daddies, not real, so she would get to do as she liked. She loved this game!

Marvin gently slid a scarf over her eyes from behind. She wondered how he had gotten the scarf; she hadn't heard any drawers get opened. She smiled deeper. That meant that perhaps this blindfolding her was a part of the plan from the beginning because John would have had to have provided the scarf before they even started. Her mind spun as she wondered when that could have happened, because Marvin had just appeared in the back yard.

She decided she didn't care. She loved being led through sexual scenarios, especially when she had zero clue of what would transpire. It was a bit scary, yet thrillingly exciting at the same time. The blindfold also ensured that very thing as well, which is why she loved it being used on her. These were all things John knew and could have likely easily shared with Marvin. The silence and inaction of the moment was driving her wild. She was hugely impatient and was ready to ask a question, but she knew better and instead stayed mute.

Marvin grabbed her by the hips and pulled her away from the window, then swiftly spun her around. She knew it was him by the smell of his breezy scent. He snatched her by the tips of her tits, yanked her forward.

She yelped out, but couldn't contain her grin. Her pussy clenched as he slightly twisted her nips as he led her along.

"Crawl onto the bed, whore," he directed in a voice that made her want to surrender everything.

She nodded and felt for the bed before climbing on.

"Hands and knees, wench, gonna fuck you until your woman velvet melts out of your pussy."

'Woman velvet', she liked that phrase! Thinking about her cum as velvet was truly sensual. Damn, he was good at seduction! She quickly obeyed and got into position.

"Then I'm going to come in you and eat you out. I want to taste our combined cum out of you, like a sex-churned feast." He fondled her breasts, then dragged his hands down her body to tease her smoldering cunt with his fingertips.

Laney was impatiently waiting for John to say something or join in the touching of her body. She sensed another person still there, but she couldn't be sure. Maybe John would head back downstairs, or maybe he'd stay in the room and watch. She hoped so. That really turned her on. Then she'd most likely get him fucking her immediately after Marvin. What she really wanted was a threesome with Marvin and John. But she knew all too well that this was John's show. He knew what she liked and often did what she wanted, but he was still the master director and coordinator.

Marvin slipped his fingers inside her quivering, wet core and began to slowly finger fuck her. It ramped up to super-fast pumping very quickly and she was close to coming within seconds.

"Good girl, getting closer now for Daddy, aren't you?" he cooed from behind.

She nodded. Talking was way too overwhelming.

Another hand pressed her clit and began to rub. That was the ticket. Like a button, she knew she was going to lose control imminently. She undulated and moaned, the added touch hurling her to the top of her O. Then another hand pressed her hip.

OMG! She startled at the three hands and then sighed. Fuck,yes! John was joining in.

"Cum for your Daddy," Marvin instructed firmly.

She relinquished control and let the orgasm consume her. She yelled without restraint. Her female muscles sent out the contractions as her body gave in. Her eyelids fluttering, her torso jerked and twitched as she came hard. She held her breath, as she was told not to during her climax. It was a bad habit, then took in a huge gulp of air and gasped loudly, her body crashing to the bed.

The hands kept riding her pussy and she launched into a second orgasm immediately. She lay on the bed helpless and spent, panting profusely. She was floating on orgasm hormones when she felt a cock tip grace her lips. Four hands were caressing her body as the cock tip pressed at her parted mouth. She opened and John inserted his cock just barely inside.

His hands caressed her cheeks and hair.

"Good girl." Only it wasn't John, it was Anderson's voice.

The realization hit her like a shit ton of bricks. Anderson had joined the room. Did that mean that John was also here? She sure as fuck hoped so! That would be the ultimate turn-on. She wanted to rip the blindfold off and scan the room to see what was really going on, but she knew she wasn't in charge, and that's exactly how she wanted it. But she was torn by wanting to disobey and just do it. Her curiosity had her quaking inside and out.

Like a passionate tug at her pleasure, Marvin rubbed his cock head along her slit. She was still on the bed helpless and sopping with hormones making her feel weak.

Anderson held the back of her head and pushed his cock into her mouth. She felt a gag coming quickly and tried to pull back, but Anderson kept on his mission and began to fuck her mouth. She gagged hard and gasped, grasping at the comforter.

Anderson groaned out, then pulled himself from her mouth. He laid down alongside her body and began to French kiss her as Marvin penetrated her pussy and began to fuck her. Anderson thrust his cock against her as they kissed, and he caressed her body before plucking at her erect nipples.

Kissing Anderson while being fucked by Marvin proved to be highly intense and she came quickly when Anderson concentrated his attention on her external clit head. She was so excited that Anderson had joined in that she could burst. It made her feel even safer with Marvin, not that she hadn't felt safe though with just Marvin. She had. He had a way about him that soothed her, kind of like John, but different somehow.

She was climaxing so many times and neither of them had yet. She knew Anderson was capable of coming several times, but he was holding off, it seemed to her. Maybe he was granting the alpha role to Marvin. That made sense to her.

Kissing Anderson was luxurious while being pounded and she came again, and again. Marvin lost it and came inside her with a roar. He slid his cock out of her and immediately dove between her legs and began to lick at her slit, slurping up all that he was fed from her still twitching hole. The aftershocks were in full force and when Marvin latched onto her clit, she raced into another orgasm once more.

Anderson removed her blindfold and gazed into her eyes with a smile. "Surprise, Laney," he whispered through his grin.

"Wow! I couldn't believe it when it was you! I totally thought it was John."

Anderson snickered then kissed her on the lips with a loud smack. "Nope. You get me."

"I always want you." She glanced around the room as Marvin rose from between her legs, his face glistening with sex juices.

He licked his lips. "Damn delicious, sweet babe."

She spied something new on the dresser. It actually looked like some kind of baby monitor; the kind she'd seen her niece have that showed a live feed of the nursery. She gasped as she brought her hand to her mouth. She pointed at it with her other hand. "That! That's new! Has John been watching this whole time?" she asked aghast.

Marvin nodded. "Yes, sweet girl. He has."

"Oh, holy fuck! That's hot as absolute fuck!" The full knowledge of it was a slow process but that sent her grin ever-growing. "Wow! Just wow!"

"I believe you are up, my dashing young man, that is, if you are, Laney?" Marvin moved away from her as Anderson rose.

"Oh, please, yes, want you to fuck me too, Anderson. Please. Pretty please. I want. I need." She had zero doubts about that!

They basically switched places, but then Anderson wanted her to rise up on her hands and knees again. Marvin slid under her and fondled and suckled her breasts as Anderson began to fuck her doggy. It didn't take long for her to climax again with Anderson railing into her bottom rubbing her G-spot while Marvin stimulated her nips and clit at once. She gasped through coming four more times before Anderson released his cum inside her well-used cunt.

She collapsed on the bed and both men settled in around her, cradling her body between them. They continued to caress her body as she floated back down from the multiple highs.

Chapter 4

She woke up in bed alone. No one was there, and instantly she was sad. She hadn't meant to fall asleep, not when she was being sandwiched by two sexy men. That just seemed so wrong!

She turned as she heard rustling in the closet. She slowly rose as she heard a hammer pounding a nail. Walking to the closet she noticed Anderson was gone, but the baby monitor was still switched to 'on' mode. She smiled, imagining John was still within earshot with it.

Marvin was standing in the closet, fully dressed, and with a hammer in his hand.

"Oh, hi," she said shyly. She stared at her toes. This was weird after he had fucked her so vigorously, but falling asleep made her feel that way, she supposed, like she was a slacker.

"Hi, sweetheart. How was your nap?" His face showed no anger at her for falling asleep. In fact, he looked extremely happy.

"Oh, so sorry I fell asleep on you guys when maybe you had wanted more sex and stuff." Well, she had, but darn her body and falling asleep like that. She scolded herself as being irresponsible and inconsiderate.

"Oh, on the contrary. You crashing like that is what warms my heart. That feeds me. Seeing you so pleasured and spent that you just fall asleep is a compliment, and a huge satisfaction to a Dom like me. It's what I strive for."

Her jaw fell slightly open. "Really?" It was hard to follow his line of reasoning, but then, she wasn't a dominant in the bedroom either, so it was a bit foreign for her to think this way.

"Yeah, totally. I want you so satiated and hormone-soaked that you just fall asleep. That's a huge key to my satisfaction, to be honest." He tilted his head as he reached for her in a hug. He kissed the top of her head. "It's what I strive for, it's not a lie. At least after I've made you come as many times as I can, that is." He raised an eyebrow. "I want you fully satiated."

She thought about the times she'd often used sex toys after John had left after sex.

Marvin really was about putting her as a priority, but just as John was now too. She was amazed at the similarities between the two, but also the differences that intrigued her.

"Have a seat against that pillow so I can tell you a story while I work." He motioned to a little makeshift bed in the only open corner of the large walk-in closet.

She felt warm and cozy as she realized what he'd set up for her. There was considerate forethought in it for her comfort and well-being, complete with a bottle of water and a cheese and cracker plate. She grinned bigger when she also spied a mint.

"I'd better pee first, then I'll settle in." Her cheeks flushed slightly. She whirled around to walk out of the closet, still feeling a bit flustered by the whole series of events that had just transpired. She peed quickly and settled into her little nest area Marvin had created for her. She scrunched up her shoulders and wiggled her toes, then relaxed. This was a new level of aftercare. He was making her feel so special, she only hoped she could convey her feelings of the same to him somehow. This man was special.

"You enjoy your snack. John and Anderson are having a happy hour drink on the patio. We will join them once I finish these shelves."

She appreciated the explanation and pulled the soft fleece blanket around her flesh. It made her cozy and comforted. The water was a welcome cool rush down her throat, and the cheese and crackers were exactly what she needed.

Marvin was pounding nails in, so she patiently waited for him to begin his story as she munched.

After a few more minutes, the hammering was done and he was able to speak. "I wasn't always the way I am now. Don't get me wrong, I've always been a dominant, but I've learned a lot over the years. My sub, who was my wife, taught me a lot, and I taught her." He smiled down at her. "It was mutual, but I needed her."

She nodded, that made sense. She popped another cheese and cracker in her mouth as she squirmed slightly. The mention of 'was' made her wonder what happened.

"You are just adorable," he said with pleasure swirling in his eyes.

She felt scrumptiously coddled. "Thank you," she said appreciatively.

"And sexy as all fuck," he added with a twinge of lust flashing across his face once more. "Anyway, I used to be more selfish. But Marge taught me a lot. She was so patient and loving. Even when I wasn't the ideal man for her. With time and experience, we fell into a dynamic together that I'd only dreamt about, read about. From what John says, you two are showing a similar path."

Laney nodded and simply said, "Yes, I think so." Bitter resentful memories from the past tried to barge into her thoughts and she shut them down.

"I always wanted to please Marge, but until I put her first, I never fully did. That's a pure fact. We also had some repairing to do in our relationship, on both ends, but I'd done more damage. I own that. No thanks to the culture I was brought up in. But I learned more patience as I aged and eventually how we had become led to her full trust in me. I'm going to stress that I was very lucky she gave me another chance, and another, and another. But I finally got it right. I became a better Dom. We were living in pure bliss." His expression turned wistful, then sad.

"What happened?" she asked with concern.

He sighed and his shoulders slumped slightly. "She got cancer." He gave her a half smile as sadness filled his eyes.

"Oh no, I'm so sorry."

"Yup, I lost the love of my life. And it about killed me. In some ways, I still think it did. But I'm still here," he said with a shrug, but also with confidence, "obviously."

Laney pulled her knees to her chest. "So, she was your sub, then?"

"Oh, yes. And I learned foreplay is every part of the relationship. Literally everything. I needed to fully support her in who she truly was, unconditionally, just as she accepted me fully. But we were also a match, if we hadn't been, we couldn't have progressed to any sort of bliss. Misalignment would have not allowed the amazing relationship we shared." His eyes were filled with wisdom. "What we had was rare."

The way Marvin was acting with her was his nature, that's why it all worked. She obviously didn't have the full trust she had with John, or even what she had with Anderson, but his demeanor and past relationship experience explained how they had meshed so well earlier.

"John has come a long way, am I right?" he inquired as if he already knew the answer.

"Yes, we didn't use to be like this at all. In fact, I thought we'd end, if I'm being honest."

"Yeah, he told me." He gave her a knowing look as if he understood.

Laney liked that Marvin knew their story. She stared up at him, feeling a bit silly at how wide-eyed she was staring at him.

"We hadn't ventured into swinging or hotwifing much, though we were headed that way. We'd go to nudist swinger campgrounds and watch others, then go off and enjoy sex for ourselves." He smiled, clearly recalling fond memories. "It was one of our favorite things to do."

"I can imagine that being wonderful too." Well, she and John had done a bit of it already, but fell quickly into the more aggressive mode of hotwifing at home right away, being it was their mutual kink. Laney smiled. "We had an epiphany, I guess."

He nodded exaggeratedly. "Yup. Every couple's journey is different, just as mine is different without her."

"Are you in search of another wife? Another ...sub?" Laney asked with genuine interest.

"Nah. I don't think I can ever top what I had with her. It's just not possible. I'll love her for eternity, regardless." He approached her and caressed her face. "I enjoyed what we did earlier, very much. Thank you for submitting to me. You didn't have to, but you chose to."

"I did choose too," she said with confidence.

"It didn't escape my notice when John came up and then when you realized it was Anderson, I saw a change in you." He stroked his chin. "Their presence made it better."

She couldn't disagree. So, John had been in the bedroom for a bit.

"It makes sense, though. It shows proof of the validity of your trust in them. I know my life will never be the same without Marge. But I can enjoy a bit of the good life on occasion."

"I'm glad you came over and I'm very happy we did what we did. I loved it very much." Flashes of what they had done filled her head and made her grin.

"Seeing you obeying and struggling to, then submitting to, my will as you came so hard and so often really tugged on my inner Dom. He hasn't made a true appearance like that for quite some time." He paused then looked directly into her eyes and stroked her cheek. "It really felt good."

He was being vague, but she didn't want to force him to give more. Instead, she chose to show how grateful she was and asked, "Is there anything else you want to do with me?"

"I'd love to make you come a few more times before we join the other two. If you are interested. But I need to get this last shelf up first." He ticked his finger in the air. "Need another job done on the books."

"Okay. Perfect." She hopped up and grabbed her plate and water.

He looked pleased. "Get your favorite toys and wait for me on the bed. If you fall asleep again, I'll just wake you."

She stopped and turned back. "Did I really sleep through you hammering nails into the wall?"

He laughed heartily. "Yes, sweetheart, you did."

"Wow. I was really conked out then. I don't usually sleep that hard." She scoffed.

"And that strokes my joy to hear." He gave her an intense direct stare. "It rages up my Dom mode, to be honest, but nothing does it like pleasuring you as you follow my instructions and submit to me, then come on command. I'm really feeling quite lucky that John approached me. Maybe sometime we can do this again."

"Oh, I'm in. I have a suspicion that John will be too."

"Yes. But it will be at his permission, of course, as it should be. But I'm happy you've given yours."

"Fully given," she declared as she almost skipped out of the closet.

She set down her plate and empty water bottle on the dresser and began to dig in her sex toy drawer in the bedside table. Her favorite clit sucker was missing, so she zipped downstairs to search for it where she thought she had left it in the kitchen. As she passed by the window above the patio, she snuck a peek outside. John and Anderson were laughing, both had cigars in their hands and a drink in front of them. Her spirit soared as she watched them for a few minutes. They were becoming such good friends.

The hammering sounds had stopped, so she quickly grabbed the sucker from the kitchen sex toy drawer and dashed up the stairs, her pussy throbbing with want.

Marvin was washing his hands in the bathroom. "Good girl. Always take the time and initiative to get what you want."

It was satisfying to have him say such things to her, affirming what she felt inside already. It wasn't coming off as condescending either, instead she rolled into a light floaty feeling, like riding on the good intentions from another person often incited.

"Got it. This one is the best. It just fits my clit the best."

"I learned a lot about sex toys with Marge. They are what helped me help her learn more about her body. I have some suggestions if you are open to them."

"Oh, my, yes! I really would love that. I'm accumulating a large collection and John is always researching new ones. He likes to spoil me with them." She scrunched up her shoulders as she allowed her eyes to fill with joy.

"Smart man," he said with a tick of his head. "We can discuss it in John's presence then, so I don't have to repeat it."

"Is it weird that I like that he's listening to us?" She swayed beside the bed, which made her breasts jiggle.

"Not at all. It also shows me you two have a very good relationship, and strong trust. You care deeply about the other's pleasure." He motioned his hand towards the bed. "Now, let's make you come five or eight more times."

She nodded and scrambled to lay on the bed, her heart all aflutter. "Yes, please, Daddy."

He smiled with appreciation as he climbed on the bed. He unzipped his pants and pulled his cock out. "Pre-fun quick suck?"

She positioned herself to take his cockhead into her mouth. She sucked him while moving her tongue around his mushroom head, then she gave firm strokes along his frenulum.

He groaned as she worked his hardness over with her mouth and fingers. His body jerked and he gently pushed her off his dick. "Thank you, baby. That was wonderful."

She lay back with a smile as he began to caress her. His hard-on bobbed as he moved and she couldn't take her eyes off it, except every once in a while to connect her eyes with his. His eyes would drift from her body to meet hers. She loved how he seemed to really appreciate her body and never stopped touching her. It was keeping her in a constant state of arousal.

He kissed her mouth, then consumed both nipples in turn all while tickling his fingers along her lower lips. She was so ready to burst into orgasm already, and this sucker toy always made her come in less than two minutes, often less than one if she was adequately aroused.

"You are a beautiful woman, Laney. You ooze sexuality and willing submission. It's a major turn-on for a Dom."

"You are very sexy too, Daddy. I love your hair, and your face, and your cock. And your hands." The sentence came out like she was immature, but she really didn't care.

He chuckled. "Well, that feels good to hear, baby girl." His facial expression turned intense. "But I'm greedy for more of your climaxes. Now, I'm going to make you come on repeat."

She squirmed as he stimulated her clitoris, her moans increasing. He pressed his fingers inside her moistened hole and her panting ramped up too. She was going to come hard and fast, it loomed at her like a full moon against a black sky.

He grabbed the clit sucker and turned it on. He popped it on and off with rapid succession, then pressed it to her engorged clit. She yelled out and her body jolted in response.

"Oh, fuck," she muttered as she twisted her head to the side and her body wiggled. This toy always owned her.

"That's a good slut, want you to give Daddy what he wants. Come on, baby girl, come on. Give it to me."

She writhed and moaned as he pressed the toy squarely to her little bean. She tried to stop the orgasm, just barely keeping it at bay a by thread. "Please," she whispered, seeking permission was one of her strongest kinks, and she was excited to exercise it with Marvin.

"Come for Daddy," he commanded.

She let the floodgates of her orgasm fall wide. The orgasm traveled through her body as it continued to emanate out of her woman parts. "Big, big, big," she chanted. The contractions became so intense she wanted to smack his hand away to give her a reprieve. "Oh, shit," she uttered. Her body scrunched and the spasms her vagina was disseminating were almost too much, but she powered through them. Overwhelmed, she let herself ride the wave to completion without smacking the toy off of her.

"I'm not stopping," he declared as he thrust his hard-on along her hip.

She wanted him to come too, but it was way too hard to say as she mounted another big O peak. Her body shuddered through it, her body lurched as 'oh fuck' responded in her brain.

"Good girl. Good girl. That looked pretty big."

She nodded with her eyes falling closed. She popped them back open quickly. No way was she falling asleep and missing anything again.

He laughed lightly and planted kisses along her breasts. He pulled the toy off.

Relief flooded her. Her pussy throbbed as she lay next to him still panting heavily.

"Float down a bit," he said in a soft comforting voice. "Then we'll go again."

He caressed her body, spending extra time on her peaked nips, nibbling and sucking them deep into his throat.

She liked that he was enjoying her boobs. She felt sleepy but fought the urge to succumb to it.

"Give Daddy one more," he said as he licked her right breast.

He laid upon her legs, pinning her down as he pressed the humming toy to her lovely engorged clit head.

She squirmed and mewled as he pressed it firmly. She escalated her sounds to signal when he'd found the perfect pressure. She launched into another monster orgasm that traveled through her body in delicious waves.

She whimpered, the intensity was ginormous this time and she almost wanted to stop.

"I've got you," he coached. "Good girl. Let it take you. That's it. That's right. Gimme. Give in. Ride that high as far and as long as you can. Awwww, so good."

The climactic journey was spectacular; the peaking orgasmic plateaus were a new experience she definitely wanted to repeat. When her body stopped undulating, he plucked the toy off. With her eyes closed, she jerked a few times as the aftershocks erupted as little bursts before dying off.

She remained silent with her eyes closed for a long time. When she fluttered them open, she smiled and said, "Wow."

Marvin was smiling at her from where he still lay across her legs and John was standing next to the bed, hands in his pockets, a proud happy grin on his face.

Chapter 5

"That was just beautiful, baby," John said with a voice full of admiration. "That looked pretty damn big."

She nodded and smiled sheepishly and scrunched up her shoulders. "Oh, it was. I almost said the safe word. It was almost too intense to bear."

"I love it when you get there. Marvin brought you there quite masterfully, I must say. It was a glorious thing to watch."

"How long were you there?" she asked, her eyes wide and her heart expectant.

"The whole time. And," he said pointing to the baby monitor, "I've seen and heard everything, as you know."

"Yes! I loved that idea! It's genius!"

"Thank you, Laney. That was a gift. You were beautiful, and even more so now with that look of utter satisfaction." Marvin climbed off Laney and started for the door. "My work here is done. I'll join the young man on the patio."

"Help yourself to the bar and snacks," John said. "And thank you, Marvin, for pleasuring my wife so amazingly. Neither of us will forget this day."

"Neither will I. I really needed it."

"We'll join you soon," John called to him as he exited the room.

John turned to her and sat on the side of the bed, stroking her right cheek as he asked, "How do you feel, baby?"

She stretched slightly and leaned into his stroking of her face. "Unbelievable and amazing, incredible, unmatched. He's an amazing man and lover."

"Good. I'm so happy. And now it's my turn, if you are up to it that is." His expression was lusty and hopeful, full of determination.

This was her favorite part of the whole thing when John would reclaim her as his. She was always floppy and cum-drunk, so the sex with John was always so deliciously otherworldly. She loved him and she loved his cock, and she couldn't wait for him to love her up with it.

"Oh, I always want you." She squirmed as jolts of want seized her. "Please, Daddy. I want you." It wasn't as weird of a thing as she had expected it would be to call Marvin 'Daddy', then minutes later call John 'Daddy'. Her brain was doing a good job of deciphering role-play for sport, and role-play for reality. John was her leader in the bedroom, and no man, no experience, or no one on Earth could ever change that. Ever.

"I'm yours, always and forever." Her cheeks felt warm, and warmth spread throughout her body as desire stirred in her loins. "Please, Daddy, fuck me." A sentence that had swirled in her head suddenly percolated out of her mouth. "A girl can only have one true Daddy."

John smiled. She hadn't seen him look this pleased perhaps ever in her marriage. It satisfied her on a level she hadn't yet been gifted. This was indeed a monumental day for them.

"Good," he said as he began to remove his clothing.

When he revealed his cock, it looked larger, fully packed to the maximum. His eyes shone with so much passion and desire as he descended upon her and nestled his lower half against her warm sopping pussy.

"Have any idea how many times you've come today?" he asked in a soft voice, leaning down upon her as if he was about to kiss her. His eyes were ablaze with mounting lust.

"No idea, it's been so many, though. I got lost in it all, so I have no idea."

"I like that," he said. "Shows you've had an amazing off-the-charts experience. And I'm so happy you did. You deserve it, my goddess." He cocked his head before saying, "And now I'm going to fuck you good and hard, pound you into this mattress."

He covered her mouth with his and kissed her so hungrily that it took her breath away. He proceeded to make love to her with such ardor and drive that she came four more times.

"I may not be able to move from this bed," she said in a slurred voice. "I'm literally drunk on dopamine, I think."

He chuckled as he cradled her body to his, kissing the top of her head in a multitude of kisses. "It's a blessing. I'm really happy I approached Marvin. I think we've both learned from him."

"Oh, absolutely I have. He's a master."

"Indeed."

They lay in silence and Laney fought the urge to fall asleep. Geez. She felt like a weak ass being so sleepy. She snuggled into John's warm body, loving the aroma of cum wafting from her.

Finally, she said, "If I don't get up, I'm going to fall asleep again. And I don't want that. I really want to sit and have a drink with everyone. Plus, I'm devilishly famished."

"Oh, babe, yeah, let's get up. I have some snacks prepared and a bottle of wine opened for you."

She dressed in a light sheer robe, choosing it for its luxuriousness and because it made her feel sexy to think about drinking on the patio in the summer air, enjoying the ambiance of the day with the three men who had just fucked her to too many orgasms to count.

John grasped her hand and pulled her along through the house, looking back at her with a giant grin every few steps. He pulled her out into the sunshine.

Both Anderson and Marvin had drinks and a plate of snacks, and happy grins across their faces.

Laney settled into the chair John had pulled out for her beside Marvin and across from Anderson.

"Sit, babe. I'll get you a plate and a glass of wine." John looked so relaxed now and she loved it.

"Love the robe, Laney. Beautiful, as always," Anderson said with a lusty grin. He had that look in his eyes like he wanted her once more and it stirred her lust again.

She almost laughed at herself for never being fully satiated, yet she felt satiated. It was an odd feeling to be full but always right on the edge of easily slipping off to being ready for more.

"Stunning," Marvin said with a pleasant face.

Sitting with them after it all was the best. She soaked up all the energy from the sun, and from all of their gratified expressions. "Now this is a party," she said in a voice loaded with satisfaction, hoping they understood how soothed she felt. Their expressions seemed like they understood, and she was pleased. Most of all, she was pleased with John, not to mention herself for trusting.

They enjoyed several rounds of drinks before the other two departed for the day, leaving Laney and John to the remainder of their aftercare.

Servicing the College Fence Builders
An Age Gap Hotwife Story

Book 5

Chapter 1

John gave Laney a wicked grin, a fully appreciative smile on his handsome face. By the look in his eyes, something was up. "I have a crew coming here today and you're helping. This is your uniform." His eyes were lit with mischief as he held up the teeny tiny red bikini. "Yours is a bit different for a construction crew," he said with a snicker.

Laney's eyes popped wider. "Oh, my Gawd! Are you serious, John? Holy shit! And construction crew?" her voice rose in disbelief. She knew nothing about construction, and he knew that. She shifted her eyes from his hand, which held a skimpy bikini top with triangles of fabric that would likely barely cover her large areolas, and G-string bikini bottoms that would be a stretch to cover her shaved mound patch. "That might be the tiniest bikini I've ever seen in my life!" She laughed with glee.

"I know, right? I searched online for it with just that description and found this steamy little number. When it arrived last week, I knew it'd be perfect for today."

Her mind spun. Okay. This has been planned for quite a while. She loved that he was planning this day for her and spending time with extreme forethought on her pleasure and involvement. Her pleasure was his pleasure, and vice versa. She was delighted to have that way of their relationship confirmed once again. But this day ahead had her baffled.

"Only, I don't know what today entails," she said with a spicy gleam in her eyes.

"Oh, you will soon. But first, you need to lie down. I'm going to slather sunscreen across your skin." He snickered. "But not over the parts," he said, emphasizing 'the parts'.

"Oh, the parts," she said with a giggle. "Yup, need to keep the parts free of chemicals."

He nodded as he gently pushed her down on the bed, lust pooling in his eyes. "Well, for that reason, and others."

He was being secretive once again, and she was beyond excited.

He began to spread sunscreen across her naked flesh with a devilish grin. "I must make sure you are fully covered. I don't want my babe getting burnt in the sunshine." He pointed at the sunshine streaming into the bedroom window. "The sun is on full blast today."

She squirmed in delight, loving his hands all over her body. "Do I get a pre-event fucking from my top man?" she asked with hope.

He shook his head. "Nope. Not happening, baby. And no toys either. You need to wait for the surprise. I want you frothing at the mouth with lust for hours before." He leaned down and kissed her pussy mound, sneaking his tongue between her clefted flesh to tweak her clit for two seconds. "All day long."

She writhed against his lick and moaned, her arousal ramping up despite his words. "Well, shit. That's certainly launching me already." She allowed her eyes to simmer down to demure. "Please, Daddy, can't my pussy lick your big cock? I can see it big and fat beneath your shorts, so I know you are ready."

His eyes twinkled. "Yes, it's big and fat, but begging won't help."

She released a guffaw in a big puff of breath. "Damnit," she muttered, truly disappointed.

He continued to rub the lotion into her skin until all the whiteness had been absorbed, and she looked her usual flesh color again.

"Fuck, this is driving me crazy, you touching me, seeing your fat cock moving beneath your shorts. Please, please, pretty please, Daddy?" she begged in desperation. She was horny as fuck, and this was sending her lust to the clouds. Well, there weren't any clouds today, she giggled to herself.

"What?" he inquired.

"Nothing, if you are keeping secrets, so am I." Though her secret wasn't likely nearly as delicious as his was, he didn't need to know that.

"Aw, baby. You know this is for you. I want you to have maximal pleasure," he insisted in an apologetic tone.

"I know. And I love you for that. But I want your cock in me. Don't you want to come in me before our guest arrives? I know you are tempted. It won't lessen my lust for whoever comes, I can promise you that." The hotwife way of like had fattened up Laney's libido better than any box of donuts ever could have. "Plus, I'll be more than hot for you after, as usual."

"I agree. This is going to blow your mind," he said with a deeply enjoying chuckle.

"You are loving teasing me, that much I can tell," she said a bit sour.

"You will not be disappointed, that much I can assure you. Now, flip over so I can make sure I fully cover your backside." The want for her in his voice was practically dripping out, yet he was denying it even to himself.

She flipped over and wiggled her ass as further enticement. That would likely get him to fuck her. He couldn't resist any form of doggy style.

He began to rub the lotion into her shoulders, arms, and back, brushing her curls aside to swipe some sunscreen across the back of her neck. He kissed the top of her head and his erection touched down against her bottom.

"Fuck," she whispered into the comforter. "Just fuck me with that already, Daddy."

"Nope," he said, with way too much enjoyment of taunting her in his voice.

He slid down her, pressing his cock for a ride down her right thigh. "Feel that? That will be your finale. It will be waiting for you all day."

What she couldn't understand was why he wanted to wait. Why not fuck her now, then fuck her again after the event? The guest surely would have her so horny for John that the after-sex would not be lesser, but amplified, as it always was after she fucked another man at John's direction.

She released a pouty, "Hmpf."

He laughed as he massaged the lotion into her buttocks.

Okay, perfect. He will lose control and fuck her. He can't resist being in position above her with his cock near her butt. But, instead, all he did was rub his clothed erection against her ass, then he scooted back to spread more lotion down her legs. He finished with the tops and bottoms of her feet.

"You put sunscreen on the bottoms of my feet?" she asked in bewilderment.

"Yup, everywhere." He stood up and her heart sank. There would be no fucking of her man now.

"That's bizarre. I can tell you I don't think I've ever coated the bottoms of my feet with sunscreen ever in my life."

He cocked his head at her with an expression of assurance. "Well, if your feet are facing up for any length of time, the bottoms could get burned."

Ah! Her second clue after the sunscreen; the sex would be outside today. "I'm putting the pieces together," she said smugly, but also acknowledging that she was mostly entirely clueless about what the day would really entail. Her quest to fuck all the work men, well, her and John's quest to have her do so, meant it would be some sort of worker. Her mind spun as she tried to think of what was broken around the house and in need of fixing or repair. She couldn't think of a single thing. The house was in immaculate shape. The pool service was fully done. Her garden and its boxes were pristine thanks to their handyman, Marvin. Her mind fixated on Marvin. He'd been so much fun to fuck. Images of his shock of white hair bobbing between her thighs and him fucking her against the front window filled her brain.

She sighed. These thoughts were not helping her horniness settle down at all. She needed a distraction. "I'm going to paint my nails and then I'll be down."

"Okay, babe. But no sex toys. I will give you a punishment if you do that. I don't want you ruining your fun by taking an orgasm pre-event."

He kept calling it an 'event' this time. That really made it sound bigger than just swinging by fucking another dude. Her mind scanned the past few days for any clues, but she had nothing. John had been very good at covering his planning tracks.

"I promise, I won't." But her mind stalled on what his punishment might be, and if she'd like it. Well, none of these thoughts were helping her passion simmer down a single bit. She released a big sigh as she began to put on the itty bitty swimsuit. It could barely be called a swimsuit; it was more like eye patches and a gauze pad than any sort of legit clothing. She imagined wearing this to the beach and hoped she'd get the chance to someday.

She laughed as she tried to get the small swatches of fabric to stay put over her nipples. It was no easy task because her every movement shifted it. She tightened the straps a bit more, and that helped it stay in place—a little better anyway. She chortled as she placed the small triangle of fabric over her mound. She couldn't get it to perfectly cover her wisps of pubic hair. No matter how she shifted it, a few strands peeked out on one side or the other.

She finally shrugged. "It is what it is. I guess whoever it is will get a preview."

She chose a nail color to compliment, a rich red, and set out to paint her toenails and her fingernails.

"Ah, painting already, nice."

He knew she was painting her nails, so his comment seemed odd to her. "Yup, almost done."

"Good. I have an omelet waiting for you on the table, so let's get that belly of yours full before you start work."

She gave him a quizzical look. She very rarely ever did handiwork around the house. He knew she was useless when it came to tools. Her mind spun around the possibilities he had planned for the day's project. Could it be some sort of reorganization? A remodel of something? But she knew she was going to be outside. Maybe he had plans to build a new firepit? Or landscaping? Landscaping. That had to be it. He knew her skill set, and using tools was not in it, but planting things was right up her alley. Maybe it was going to be a new flower garden next to her vegetable garden. Or perhaps a new sitting area with tall shrubs and flowering bushes.

They made their way to the kitchen.

She sat at the table across from John. "I think I know what it is I will be doing today," she said confidently after chewing a bite of omelet.

"Oh, yeah?" he asked with a raised eyebrow and a skeptical look. "Do tell." His amused smile didn't infuriate her at all, because she was right.

"Landscaping. Or a new flower garden," she said with full confidence.

He laughed heartily, shook his head, and said, "Nope. It's not that."

"Fuck," she muttered as the omelet settled in her belly. John was right on the big breakfast; she never liked to fuck on an empty stomach because she always ended up focusing on her hunger and couldn't fully enjoy the pleasure. He knew her so well, and she loved that he did. Her mind disobeyed her resolve to move on and drifted to when it hadn't been so. A time in their marriage when, if he knew, he just hadn't cared enough, or valued her enough, to act on it. She'd felt neglected, unimportant, and worst of all, unsexy to John. But all had blissfully changed, right when, on the verge of divorce, he had completely transformed, and the new way of life they were both enjoying had finished the transformation. He'd become the best husband, lover, and dominant man in the bedroom she could have ever hoped for. Sure, he had room for improvement, but each experience, each day, brought more of that to fruition. She couldn't even imagine reclaiming those old feelings of wanting to divorce him again. They were now so foreign to her that, at blissful moments, even the memory of them faded to nothingness. Well, almost. The stain of them would forever be there, unfortunately.

The best part of it all was she and John had become friends again. Best friends. They'd never really had that, she surmised now that she enjoyed his presence. They were on an even playing field. Well, actually, he put her first, and that solidified everything. He got exactly what he wanted, and she was given what she wanted first. And he'd embraced the role of director and leader, shedding any contaminating debacle of jealousy. The whole thing mystified Laney, but she couldn't be happier. Her old life was becoming more like some horrible movie she'd watched when younger, or a friend's life rather than her own.

"John. I know you're amazing, and you are loving this whole game, but I'm dying to know. But I also admit, I'm loving the surprise too. I'm just super impatient."

He rubbed his hands together. "Well, you won't have to wait long now."

She jumped up and clapped her hands, which made her unsupported large breasts flop.

"Wow. Do that again in about fifteen minutes and you will love the reaction you get." He scooped up all the dishes and nodded to the backyard. "You go out and lay on a lounge chair. Don't swim. Save that for later. I'll clean up. The arrival time is approaching."

Chapter 2

She scrambled outside, sunglasses and beach towel in hand, flip-flops secure on her feet. She definitely wanted her toes showing after taking the time to paint them to perfection.

Her heart pitter-pattered as she scampered out the basement door into the bright sun. It was so exciting to be on the verge of not only sexual bliss, but turning John on too that her body was ablaze with anticipation. Her heart was beating fast, and the blood was warming up her body as much as the sun's rays. After just a few minutes, she was getting hot, and the pool was looking tempting. It would be so refreshing. Lots of bare wet skin was always a turn-on, so she rationalized to herself that being wet would ignite the visitor's passion higher as she dipped her toes into the pristine water. She slipped her foot in deeper to the arch of her heel, but froze when she heard several male voices approaching.

The side gate door swung open and five men, who looked to be in their twenties, entered. They were all dressed in paint-stained, worn clothing, and two of them carried large buckets, others had brushes and rollers, and the last two carried a fence door. Tools hung secured from their work belts, framing their crotches, which were free of hanging tools. How perfect. She'd never realized what a nice showcase tool belts made for cocks until just this moment.

Her face spread into a grin as waves of excitement burst inside her. This was going to be a gang effort, and she was likely going to be pleasured almost out of her mind with orgasms from strong young men. Her heart danced into the sky.

John emerged from the basement sliding door. "Welcome, my friends. I'm so happy to give you all a job to help supplement paying for school."

Laney had no doubt that John had offered them a generous amount of money. Not having kids of their own, they had a lot of money, and John always embraced more donations in his new skin. Another bonus of the new John. At times, she barely even recognized his doings because he'd changed so much from his past self. It was all a blessing. And she'd changed too. They were both so much happier it was almost scary to think how miserable they both used to be. Everyone said people don't change, but she'd seen a testament to the opposite firsthand.

"John, I can't thank you enough. When my dad said you were looking for help, I was pretty excited. I had two more friends lined up too, but they had to back out last minute, so hopefully the five of us will be enough for this job today."

"No worries, it will be good." He swung his arm towards Laney. "Plus, you have the help of my lovely wife, too."

That was laughable, but no one laughed. Instead, all the men took in Laney's body with intent gazes. The hunger in their eyes fed her desire and she was already ready to have them riding her wet holes. Just like that. She was feasting on the lascivious looks on their faces and their bodies were over the top in peak shape. It was all enough foreplay on its own to make Laney wet. Her lower lips were already dribbling wetness and blossoming into arousal as she shifted her thighs so they would caress against each other. She suppressed a moan as she smiled at the sexy men.

"Hi, nice to meet you. I've been so curious about what I'd be doing today." Her tone was innocent and perky.

The dark-haired tallest one chuckled under his breath and not a single man in her back yard lacked a giant grin.

She was on cloud nine, knowing John had likely already prepped them, and her clit twitched. She imagined how they'd all tangle into an aggressive body pumping orgy and the joy almost made her lightheaded.

The one who had spoken with John, with dark blonde wavy hair and a dimple, said, "It's a pleasure to meet you, Laney. I'm Lance. John has told us a lot about you, and I must say, you are a vision to behold. You exceed even his incredible description of you."

"You can tell her exactly what you think. She won't get offended. Instead, it turns her on more. So don't hold back." John cocked his head at them and raised his hands. "I'm not kidding. And as I mentioned, she loves to be talked to dirty. The dirtier the better."

The young men all looked even happier at that statement, but none said a word.

"We will have rules, though. I will be working in the basement by that window right there. And I will periodically come out to check on you all to see the progress, and to assess my wife. You may touch her wherever and whenever you like. Is this okay with you, Laney?"

She nodded vehemently. "Please, and thank you," she said eagerly. She waited with bated breath for John to spill the rest of the conditions. But her mind wandered as John motioned for Lance to approach him. John began to whisper in Lance's ear.

She was dying to know what he told him.

The other men's big grins got larger, and their eyes were blazing into pyres of combustion. They looked hungry, their sex drives luminating out of them in droves. Their smoldering looks scintillated Laney's motivation, her inner goddess burning brighter with vivacious elation. She was going to fuck these men into her topmost cum drunk intoxication, harnessing them into their own blissful satiation, which she'd reap the benefits from. Sure, they'd get to enjoy her body and come, but with this many cocks, she would be the one deliciously riding the sexual Mount Everest of a crew like this. She'd been wanting a multiple experience for quite some time, and the fact that John deemed it worthy to satisfy this on her sexual bucket list made her love him even more. John was rolling nicely into the getting off on delivering Laney her sex life's greatest fantasies, and that alone made her want to gift him all of his.

And that these were young men was also exciting to her. She'd get the benefit of their fit bodies as they thrust into her. She was ready to fuck, nothing else needed to happen, and all they'd done so far was walk in and smile at her with lusty looks. She adored that they were revealing their want for her in their expressions, not like out in the real world where everyone had to shroud their lust for others.

This was going to be hot. And likely blow Laney's brain and hormones to the moon. She had zero doubts.

John looked ready to address the group. "When you're doing the painting stage, I want you all to take turns touching Laney's body as you work. Leave your paint handprints on her flesh as evidence. I'd love to see her body completely covered in white paint by the time you all finish the job. But the rule is, it has to be just a press of your palm. You can't swipe your hands down to coat her in paint to accelerate this. Once she's fully covered in paint, it's time to fuck."

They all chuckled in delight, some of them joking with each other quietly amongst themselves as they were clearly realizing how raunchy this was and that it was legit happening. They were elated, like they were just learning of a good and massive fortune they were being presented with.

Her feelings matched.

"And Laney, you cannot add any paint to your own body to hurry this along. I will be watching you, as will they. I know you are very hungry to fuck these guys, but you must wait, and it will be at their pace, and mine." He grinned like a demon who had his prey cornered and would fully dictate their fate. "They are going to extend your edging along as long as possible until you are so ravenously livid, you'll want their cocks so bad. But you don't get to try to seduce them to hurry this process up, other than using your words in response to what they do to you and to flirt. I've given them instructions on how to please you, on the timing of how I want the day to go, and how it will all go down at the end. Your job is to help where they tell you to help, and enjoy the pleasure of flirting with them, with the knowledge that they are going to fuck you into so many orgasms you might collapse into a dreamland coma state right in our backyard."

The promises of ecstasy thrilled Laney. If Laney wasn't already a wanton horny whore, now she was in a tumultuous sex-starved fever, and all she wanted to do was strip each of these men down to nakedness and let them maul her into a wild orifice riding spree, an all-out overindulgent circus of sex that would launch her into the most scrumptious debauchery she'd ever known. This was going to be epic, and John was the man to give it to her. He knew exactly how to win with her and it secured her hooks deeper into him as much as his were entrenching deeper into her.

She jumped up and down, making her generous breasts chug up and down her body.

The men catcalled and whistled, so she jumped more. She adored being objectified, when she desired it, which was when she felt safe, and she most certainly did with these robust-looking men under John's command. She could see erections had already formed for most of them. All she wanted to do was unzip their shorts and pull out their man meat, rub her cheeks along them, dragging precum down their hard shafts with her face. Then she'd take them each into her mouth to wet them before they'd stick them into her lush core and ride her until her screams rang out loud enough to knock down the fence they were here to fix. She couldn't believe her most amazing fortune that this unforeseen experience was within grasp, looming at her like yummy leering. She never understood why women didn't like a man looking at them with want. It literally lit her up like a forest fire. And the more, the better.

"Okay, are there any questions?" John scanned the young men, a humorous grin permanently fixed on his face. "I know if someone had given me this opportunity when I was your age, I'd have thought I'd won the lottery. And you are very welcome." He chuckled wholeheartedly.

They all nodded and agreed.

Laney raised her hand. "I have a question."

"Okay, baby, what is your question?"

"Can I take off my ... uniform?" she asked hopefully.

"Nope. You definitely cannot be the one to remove your uniform." John's tone was authoritative, and she sensed this was not something he'd forgive if she didn't follow his command on it.

"I adore your uniform," the dark-skinned man said with a lustful grin.

"Yeah, I don't think any establishments outside of strip clubs or brothels would ever consider this any sort of uniform." She giggled with relish. She rang her fingers over the little patches of fabric covering her erect nipples, her excitement at being their sexual plaything blooming further. Despite the hot sun and not even being touched, her nipples had not flattened out to a calm state the entire time the men had been there.

"Now you know why I avoided your parts with sunscreen. No one wants to taste that shit," John said with a deeply lecherous chuckle, his smirk never lessening, even as he reached for the door handle. "Oh, wait, let's do introductions first. Lance, you know."

"I'm Lance, as I already said," Lance said with a curt nod, his bright blue eyes sparkling.

"Jelson," said the dark mocha-skinned man with a salute.

"Mason," said the tall, dark-haired one with a bob of his head and a luscious smirk.

"Alex," said a thin man of medium height, lean muscular body, and a goatee, who so far had the largest bulge at his groin.

"Shane," said the body builder guy, who was stocky with thick muscles, whom Laney thought would be fabulous at holding her in the air while he fucked her.

Their bodies held surprises and promise for the orgy ahead.

She spread her arms wide, up and away from her body. "And I'm Laney," she said with joyful blushing gracing her cheeks. "Hotwife at your service," she proudly declared.

"Oh, yes, you are," Jelson said with deep appreciation and salaciousness filling his tone.

"Alright, I'm off to work, and so are all of you. Come in for water and snacks. I have the bar and the bar counter loaded. So, help yourself anytime. It's going to be very hot. Make sure you all stay hydrated. And if anyone wants to take a dip in the water, do it quick and before the painting phase starts." He smirked. "I can't wait to see my wife all coated in handprints. You know your tasks. Let's go."

Laney nodded with a grin; she was so ready for the same. Her pussy lips wetted, thinking about all those touches she'd soon enjoy. She was so excited for the day she could burst. So that's what he was doing while she was waiting in the backyard, getting all the snacks set up, which he must have had ready in the bar fridge. He was the most amazing man who was exceeding even her biggest dreams these days. She was blessed, and he was making sure of it. Just when she thought he couldn't shock her more with his awesome plans, he topped it. She mused how he may likely help her uncover new fantasies and kinks she didn't even know yet that she had.

The men started setting up their gear. She scanned their firm, healthy-looking bodies, taking in their toned and muscled frames, and began to imagine how each would fuck. She literally could no longer look at a man and not imagine how he'd fuck. Her brain would launch into daydreams of sex in the timeframe of less than a heartbeat. No man in public or private was safe from the sexual viper of her imaginative sex drive.

Jelson had skin that reminded her of molten chocolate. She literally could not wait to see his cock and feel it inside her body. He had a direct intense gaze that spilled out horniness.

This game was ideal and she'd get to flirt, touch, and be touched by them all day long. It was like the best possible pampering of her sexuality she could possibly imagine, short of being in an actual spa with these men.

Jelson handed Laney a hammer and a tool belt. "For you, my very sexy woman, we need to gear you up for work." He grinned deeply and she adored how his white teeth contrasted with his glistening dark skin.

"Jelson, right?"

"The one and only," he smirked.

He was a very sexy man, and she was fighting the urge to touch him, until she realized that she didn't need to resist that urge. She was allowed to, and he was interested in that as well. She smiled at him as she reached for the belt.

"Help me put it on?" she asked coyly with flirty eyes, anything to entice his arms around her was her goal.

"It would be my most excellent pleasure to assist you." He took the belt from her and reached around her body to secure it to hug her hips.

She put her hands on his biceps, then migrated them to his chest, savoring the bulky muscles bulging out from his loose workout tank top. He immediately reciprocated and pressed his fingers into her hips with a slow caress of his fingertips. A lingering touch that his eyes told her was filled with want for her.

She almost muttered 'yes please and now'.

"Need to tighten this a bit, it's rather large for you," he chuckled as he ran his hands to the back of her, feeling up her buns unnecessarily in the process.

"Oh," she cooed. "I like how you tighten things up." She rose up on her tippy toes as he groped her bottom.

He released a bubble of laughter. "Speaking of tight..." his voice trailed off as he gripped her ass cheeks even harder in a demanding squeeze. "I love your nice tight butt." He pressed his pelvis to her mound, and his erection felt hefty.

She mused he must be an ass man with that blatantly lewd look across his handsome face.

He tightened the belt along her hips, not missing a single extra touch of her flesh. "You look very sexy in a tool belt. What do you think guys, is she ready?"

"Oh, for sure, very sexy. A woman in a bikini with a tool belt is about one of the sexiest images I can imagine personally, short of being flat-out naked with one," Alex mused with a sexy grin. "I think I've got my online search terms for later."

The man next to him, Shane, chuckled with a nod. "No doubt. And same."

Laney giggled in delight. "Well, I'm sure that might legit happen for you all here."

"Oh, but not for quite some time," Lance said. "John has told us we can't remove your swimsuit until he gives the go-ahead." A rule follower, but she guessed they all needed to be to get the prize.

She pouted. She really was willing to work in the nude. Though she supposed that may not work if someone were walking behind the fence on the path. They might call her into the police or something lame like that. She snorted softly. It's not like this little of a bikini was going to protect her skin, it was basically just hiding her nips and pussy mound with no other purpose. Her ass was basically fully on display for them. But she loved that.

She pursed her lips. "He's a party pooper." Well, that wasn't exactly true. He'd created this amazing scenario. She'd just have to be patient to be naked, as would the men have to be patient to see her nude. "So, what does my incredible hubby have us doing? I see a new gate as well."

"Yup, a new gate will be installed, a few fence repairs, rebuilding a few sections, then painting the new gate and a coat across the whole thing."

"Wow. That will take the whole day. We will be too tired to fuck," Laney exclaimed as she ran her gaze along their enormous fence.

The men all laughed and snickered.

"That's literally not possible," said Lance as if it were the funniest joke he'd ever heard.

Each man agreed with a giant grin.

"We're going to fuck you really good, Laney. Don't you even worry your gorgeous little goddess self about that. We will be more than ready to fuck you even after this long day," Alex said with a salacious grin. "We have lots of energy."

She again enjoyed taking in the delightful vision of their youthful bodies. She had zero doubts he wasn't right. She relished the filthy thoughts of them all going at her body like sex-crazed fiends, like men starving to taste her, ravage her, destroy her into a mountain of unstoppable climaxes, and it made her body quiver as she took in a deep breath. Her heart was beating faster at the mere thought of their upcoming union. They'd fuck her right on the spot if they could see into her brain.

She twisted her toe slightly. "I guess I'd better remove these high heels so I can get down to work."

"Please don't," Jelson begged. "I am really enjoying the sight of that." He grinned and licked his lips. "You look delicious."

Her cheeks flushed. More compliments. She'd be so full of sexy feelings by the end of the day, she'd be ripe to orgasm into double digits for sure. "Okay, I'll leave them on, but they might make me less helpful. But I'm going to need your guidance in all this. I'm afraid I'm not very good with these kinds of tools." That brought on more imaginings of them, all taking turns standing behind her, pressing their cocks to her buttocks as they helped her use tools. She speculated once more that John was a magical sexual scenarios genius. "Where do you want me?"

"A woman in a bikini using tools and helping? I don't think my cock can get any harder," said Shane with a leering, lingering glance at Laney's body. "It's like watching women lift weights at the gym. It's just sexy as fuck." He motioned for her to come to him. "Come here, sexy. Let's get started on removing this old gate."

She sauntered over to him as her mind fixated on him. He was very strong-looking, the strongest-looking one in the group due to his really thick muscles. Her brain scattered in a million directions when he pulled her against his heavy body.

"This is going to be really fun," he whispered into her ear. "To be given permission to touch a sexy woman like you all day long is just wow. Especially knowing we are building up to fucking you." He cackled wickedly. "I'm going to have a hard time concentrating on the work. My dick is already full for you. I can't wait to fuck you, Laney."

Shivers ran all over her body as she sensed his strength as he clutched her to him. "Wow, I'm so turned on, I wish we could fuck now. I'm so ready to feel you inside me." Permission to think and speak her mind was a gift John had also given her with their new way of life. And it extended out of the bedroom, too. Their love had become unconditional. But she also knew she'd never hurt John. There was an extra protection in that with how they now were. They gave each other full freedoms, and that created an environment in their marriage of an even stronger desire to not only please each other, but be careful with each other's hearts. It was not something that she expected to happen, but it was one of the most beautiful things about their new way of being a couple.

He pressed her back with both his hands and pressed his forehead to hers. "May I kiss you, Laney?"

She nodded eagerly.

He pressed his open mouth to hers and slid his tongue in. She responded by caressing her tongue along his and they fell into a deep French kiss. He leaned into her and lifted her off the ground, literally sweeping her off her feet as he intimately kissed her. The others hooted as they stayed lip-locked kissing for several minutes. He thrust his hard erection against her body and her arousal catapulted upward.

She moaned into his mouth as they continued to make out.

He broke the kiss and released her, muttering, "Shit, I'm so ready now."

She was panting heavily, the making out with him in front of the other men had her lust at peak point. "Me too, oh this is going to be so hard to wait all day long."

"Whew, shit. I've got to focus." He peeled his eyes from her slowly as she returned his horny look.

"Okay, let's do this." She was as determined as he was to follow the plan.

Laney, Alex, and Jelson set to work on the gate while the others went over to the corner near the garden to repair a broken-down area of the fence there. Music suddenly blared from the pool house. Laney glanced over and saw her husband coming out the door of it.

"Nice kiss," he called with applause. "Very sexy." He gave a double thumbs up.

The music changed the mood and Laney felt like it was more of a party than a workday as she flirted, enjoyed their frequent touches, and all their attention as she did minor things they directed her to do. She loved them telling her what to do as well. It was the whole male dominance thing, which was only working because it was tied to the promise of them fucking her later. Though honestly, she seemed more in the way than any real help, but they kept insisting the things she was doing were helping. She figured holding tools and handing them out when needed was actually help. She'd hold a board here, retrieve a screw there, and before she knew it, she was thirsty for some water.

"Water break," she announced. "Can I bring anyone a bottle of water?" This was truly a way she felt useful as well.

They all raised their hands to her.

She nodded and made her way into the house to snag water bottles for all. Inside the blast of cool air chilled her sweaty skin in a flash. She drew in a refreshing breath as she saw her husband sitting at his desk. "Hi, everyone needs water, so I'm the water girl."

He gave her a pleasant expression. "Well, you're my girl first." He motioned her over.

"Yes, I am," she said as she straddled his lap, grinning flirtatiously.

"You wear a tool belt very nicely, babe." He pulled her body as close as possible and pressed the back of her head so their mouths could meet.

She squirmed on his lap as they kissed, rocking her pelvis against his hard erection. "Mmm, you taste and feel incredible."

"As do you," he said in a breathy voice as he fondled her ass and hips.

"Wanna fuck? We could do a quickie."

He slapped her right ass cheek. "No no no. You must wait, my horny little bitch." His wicked grin told her he loved giving her that little spank as a display of confirming his dominance over her.

She truly loved submitting to him. A feeling that, if someone had asked her about it years ago, she'd deny was ever possible with John.

"Yes, Daddy," she said as she crushed his hard dick with her pubic bone. "If you say so."

"You certainly aren't making that easy," he said with humility, but pleasure danced in his eyes, regardless. "You having fun?"

"Oh yes, you've outdone yourself with this. A whole day of flirty edging with sexy as fuck big strong men with the promise of an orgy at the end? That's like the biggest dream a girl like me could ever hope for." She narrowed her eyes. "You really should direct porn. You have a serious talent for this."

He nodded. "I know, right? And I love it. But for your pleasure." He slapped both her ass cheeks at once hard. "Now get that bubble butt of yours back out there with waters for these strapping young men before I pull you over my knee for disobeying. They need fluids to coat you with their cum. Keep 'em hydrated babe so you get their cum."

She threw her head back in a devilishly torrid laugh as she rose off his lap. He added another slap to her butt before she was out of reach.

"Hey," she said teasingly. She'd been wondering if she should bring an impact play act up with John, just to try it once.

"Hey yourself, it wouldn't take much for me to pull you over my lap, and you know." He heckled her as he slapped the air.

"Oh, don't I know it." She glanced at her backside to see if his smacks had left handprints. Her buns were only barely pinkish. A deep lusty pull of arousal squirmed itself into awareness deep from a secret hidden place in her gut. Part of her loved the idea of going back out to the men with a red freshly spanked ass, but that was a kink for another day, perhaps... a maybe that was feeling more and more like a yes.

She shook her head to reorient her to focus to the current kinks happening instead. She pressed the cold water bottles to her breasts so she could carry all six and made her way back outside, after giving John a reticent smile.

Chapter 3

She delivered all the men their waters, and each one thanked her with either a kiss or a grab. This was her idea of the best day ever, being fondled, suckled, attended to, and flirted with all day long by multiple men. It hardly seemed possible that she was being gifted this epic day.

Her mind wandered as she helped install the gate. Physical labor wasn't something she hated, but she worried she might be too tired to fuck by the end of the day. Sucking dick was something she wanted to do while they worked, and she made plans to make that happen at some point when it seemed right. She wanted to give them pleasure and she yearned to please them.

She fell easily and swiftly into their team camaraderie and found herself enjoying them, the banter, the joking around—because they didn't hold back even with her in their presence. They experienced the accomplishments together too. It was like they were forming relationships, which Laney guessed would make their enjoyment of what they'd do at the end of the day even more fantastic. She truly liked these men. They were honest, hardworking, and they included her. They wouldn't have had too. They could have just treated her like eye candy, and while she loved being eye candy as part of her exhibitionistic kink, she also loved feeling like a member of their team.

"How many fences do you guys work on over the summer? I'm assuming it can only be over the summer with school." She handed Jelson another screw by hugging him snuggly from behind.

"Ah, that feels so good. Love your tits pressed to my back," he slurred.

He was very sweaty, but Laney didn't mind one bit. She knew he'd be fucking her with that sweaty body later, smearing sweat across her flesh as their bodies tangled, so what was a little sweat now?

"Yup. We all come home over the summer to do this fence business, then head back to school. But I'm afraid we are going to lose some of us to internships next year, so this might be our last full summer crew," Lance said as he bent Laney over slightly and humped her butt.

She laughed in delight, musing this would never happen anywhere in the world but in her backyard on a day like today. She savored their boldness, that they were doing whatever they wanted to her. She smiled hugely each time to reconfirm for them they could take such sexual liberties with her, and not only were they welcomed, but desired. It was an all-out sexual innuendo and sexual advances playground, and they were all taking full advantage of it.

"Ah, yeah, that is a bummer. It's the last hurrah for you all." She twerked her ass backward grinding it into his firm hard-on. It almost felt like a cheesy porno, but a guilty pleasure at once.

"Yeah, we actually formed as one of the crews after our sophomore year in high school. Since it's my dad's company, we could do it. And we've been fence builders, repairers, and painters every summer since. It's been a great money maker for us and for the company."

"So, I assume you will be working for your dad after graduation?" She watched him play with a tape measure, grinning at him thinking his toying with it was kinda cute. She went back to twerking against Lance's groin and he smacked her bottom.

She squealed and launched forward. When she glanced back, she savored his naughty grin.

"Yeah, I'll eventually take over the company, but yeah, my major is business management in preparation for that." He rubbed her flesh where he'd hit her, then released her.

"It must be nice knowing you don't even have to search for a job out of college." She toyed with her own hammer as she watched the other two men swing the gate. It flowed freely and matched up to the fence perfectly. They were skilled at this, and it was more fun than Laney had expected it would be.

"Yeah, it really is. Now I just need to find the right partner and I'll be set for life." He winked at her. "I'd be more than lucky to find someone like you."

She loved that they were attracted to her, especially being that they were young men, and she was old enough to have easily been their mother. The whole age gap thing was a turn-on and being desired by any man was a turn-on to her, no matter their age, but to be desired by these guys was not something she had really expected to happen. She understood the whole MILF phenomenon, and she had loved sex with Marvin being younger than him, so she shouldn't be surprised, but there was just something extra about this that she doubted she'd ever top this experience. This was a once-in-a-lifetime chance. But honestly, that didn't matter. All her hotwife experiences were divine and she loved that John got into it too. Her mind wandered as she wondered if any of them had girlfriends. Sexy men like them would likely have women, but perhaps they were in open relationships or between relationships, but it wasn't her place to question, or even ask. They were grown men, and she was taking them at that, despite their youth, they were still making their own decisions as adults. It was crazy to think that she could have parented them, though, these people who were full-grown men with their own sex drives, libidos, and wants. They most certainly were not boys, they had fully invested stock in the scrumptious maturity of manhood. And fat cocks beneath their clothes to prove it.

"So, what do you do for work, Laney?" asked Jelson with genuine interest. She had the urge to run her fingers over his lush puffy-looking hair.

"I used to work at a big job, yep, I was a corporate big wig, but I got laid off. Now I'm a housewife and a hotwife. I'm proud of it and super happy. I take care of our home, cook all homemade meals, work out every day, and," she snickered, "I take care of and fuck John at least once a day."

"Wow, now that's the life," he replied. "As long as you are both happy with it, that is."

"Oh, we're both so happy now. We don't need the money, John makes so much. And we don't have kids, so we haven't spent a lifetime spending money on anyone but ourselves and our house, so our pockets are very fat. But recently, with all this cooking, I've started working on creating a cookbook to publish." She gave him a proud smile.

"Oh yeah? An entrepreneur too. That's pretty cool," he said with a big white toothy grin. "Sexy, loving, horny, creative, and smart. And a hotwife. You are the full package. My ideal woman." He grinned at her as a chuckle rang deep in his throat. "I feel I can say that to you. Not to make you feel like a woman has to be a package, but you've got it all. A dream woman."

She beamed. That was a compliment she likely wouldn't ever forget. "Monogamy was no longer working for us, I guess. But if you asked me years ago, I didn't see this coming at all. In fact, I thought we'd part ways, eventually." Her expression went solemn; she didn't want to further elaborate. She lamented that her past always had to make an appearance to plague her at some point, but she quickly swiped it away in an attempt to not fall fully into those feelings on such an exciting day. "But we are in such a different place now. It's like we've entered an alternate universe. This lifestyle really pumped life into our sex life and our marriage. It's kind of shocking, really." She paused. "But we had to be in a better place first, or this whole hotwifing thing wouldn't have worked."

"Interesting. I saw a dude speak on this once. He was a full supporter of ethical non-monogamy. He said there's even scientific evidence that competition spurs things along. He said sperm count even goes up in men in open marriages, the attitudes change, and both members of the couple try harder for each other, like with romance and support and shit like that." He shrugged. "Kinda makes sense though. And not to be a lazy ass but value your partner more legit, ya know? Makes ya work for it."

"Yeah. Totally. Wow. I've literally never heard this. I need to do an internet search later and read up on the sperm count thing. Biological evidence. Huh. That's pretty amazing." Laney's mind started to dwell on things again, but she didn't want that to happen, so she reached up and ran her fingers over Jelson's hair. "I like your hair, it's like, spongy."

He chuckled gregariously and his grin lingered thereafter as he fondled her hair. "I like your hair, too, sexy. It's beautiful. Feels so nice between my fingers." He pursed his lips. In a more aggressive tone, he declared, "And I can't wait to take a grip of it when I get to fuck you from behind."

He thrust his hard-on against her bare belly and she melted. Her clitoris chirped. Her lust was in the red and ready to burst out the top of her head like fireworks she wanted that so badly.

"I am drooling for that. I'm so ready to fuck you guys, it's unreal." Her passion was raging to all-out vulgar at this point. It was the same feeling she got when she knew she'd push her boundaries further than ever before.

John popped out of the sliding door and waved. "Hey all, how's it going out here?"

The guys on the other end of the yard waved. One of them hollered, "Making progress, sir. Going good."

"Getting close to the painting phase soon, I see," he yelled across the yard as he made his way over to assess their work.

Laney smiled up at Jelson. "I'm very eagerly waiting for you to do that to me. And just so you know, my hair makes an excellent ponytail. Just ask John. And by the way, when you said that it made my clit twitch."

He pumped his fist. "Yes, love to hear that, sexy."

"Let's get this shit done so we can do that," he said in a determined voice. "Your man really knows how to get us going. I was already ready to fuck you the moment I saw you, but now, I'm flat-out beast mode for it."

She giggled. "I'm pretty sure I'll love your beast mode."

"Whew, I may get a bit rough, to be honest. But according to John, you got a kink love for that, amiright?"

"Yes," she said nodding aggressively. "I do. I love the entire gradient. I just love fucking."

"Ah, girl, you are something else." He guffawed and dragged her back to their current job where Lance and Alex were re-doing a section of fence that had broken off from a tree falling on it last month.

They worked for another twenty minutes. They all looked to Laney like they were melting, they were all dripping wet with so much sweat. Clearly, the afternoon heat was getting to them all and they needed a cool down, the water bottles weren't cutting it.

"Group swim!" Laney announced with a raise of her hand, realizing she was the only one in a swimsuit.

"I'm in," Jelson was the first to say, but they all followed suit, making their way to the pool.

Laney made a beeline for the water too, wishing she could strip her suit off and skinny dip, but John's words rang in her head. She'd have to wear it this time. She walked into the water with a huge sigh. "Feels amazing, guys. Better jump in."

She watched in utter delight as the men stripped down to their underwear and her world was transformed into a hot guy adult film shoot. She could see everything, including those sporting full erections at the moment. Her lust seethed and hissed, ready to snap at them like a snake bite.

They didn't hesitate but jumped in, doing cannonballs, dives, or simple plops. She smiled at their boyish jubilance and felt their playful energy meld with hers. Her body filled with glee as she moved about in the water amongst them.

"Aw, damn, this feels so incredible. I needed this," said Shane before diving underwater.

"Whew," Alex said as he popped up out of the water and shook his head, making the water spray off his hair before it settled against his scalp. "That was well timed. I was ready to melt out there in that hot sun."

"It's a scorcher," Laney said with a nod.

Lance grabbed Laney from behind and she squealed. He pulled her body snug to his and nestled his erection between her buns. He began to thrust, which tugged slightly at her G-string, arousing her further. He nibbled her ear and she leaned into him.

"I had to take a bite, you look incredible wet," he slurred sexily into her ear.

She writhed in his touch, trying to feel up every part of his body with her own. "Geez, if John hadn't stated the rules, we'd be fucking now."

"I know, you're right," he said in a low sexy voice. "This is an exercise in extreme patience, but it's got me hotter than fuck to ravage you."

Mason snuggled in along her front side and snatched her mouth in a kiss.

Play time in the pool had them all owning the foreplay as Jelson swam close as well as Alex. The four of them fondled her body. It was a taste of the ecstasy to come, but Laney was all-out ready to disobey John and beg the men to fuck her right now. She was fire alarm status hot for them and she wanted their cocks up and in her wet holes.

"Fuck," she muttered as hands caressed her breasts, ass, hips, face, and neck. Hands were everywhere on her, making her lust a randy primal creature she wasn't sure she could control. "I want your cocks in me so bad, I'm ready to burst into flames."

"Same," Jelson mimicked with as much intensity.

"Get her all worked up, then stop," John instructed sternly from the side of the pool. "Get yourselves so edged you can barely stand it, then pull back. Yeah, just like that. Nice, very nice."

Laney wanted to pummel John. This push-and-pull tease with so many men had her emotions frothing. She could barely stand it.

"Oh, my Gawd. Please, more. John. Please," was all she could manage to say as the men brought her to the brink of her tolerance.

Jelson was the first to pull away, and the other men followed suit.

She panted all alone in her solitary space in the pool. She darted her eyes wildly between them, then she swiveled her eyes to John. "This sucks ass," she screamed.

He chuckled as did the men, which made her laugh at herself.

"Trust me, you all will be thanking me later today," John said with a laugh riddled in his words. "And you know very well, this applies to me too because I'd love to charge into it too, but, patience will have its own big rewards."

John had taken to loving edging her to the point where she'd literally beg for his cock. And he was right, it made their sex better, hotter, like a raging inferno on steroids. It drove the passion higher to be forced to wait. Dwelling on the rise, the road to the rise, and the forced pull back was something Laney found brought her to ravenous she-beast better than any other tactic John employed with her. Orgasm control was hot, and he had learned how to expertly wield it with her. But this...this day was likely his masterpiece.

"I want to beat you," Laney joked.

This got the men laughing at her, as did John.

She laughed too. "It's funny, but I'm not kidding."

"I know, baby, but take a look at how passionate this is making you."

"Hmpf," she said as she dove under the water. She needed coldness to flood her body, but it did nothing to simmer down her wanton, whorish self. She wanted to be fucked, and she wanted it now. Brat mode was rearing its head and she needed to temper herself back to not ruin this day. Plus, John was in charge. And that's how she wanted it.

She emerged from the water and stood up. "Well, I'm most certainly hangry for sex, but this is your plan, John, and I'll follow it." She swam over to the edge of the pool and pressed her body to the wall. She caressed his toes as he looked down at her, his arms crossed over his chest, and a devilish smile plastered across his face.

"I love you, babe," he said in a sweet voice.

"I love you, but this is driving me crazy."

"I know," he said with a smug expression. "Just think about how amazing all those cocks will feel later, and how much more satiating it will be having had to wait for it."

He wasn't wrong, but she was impatient. She laid her face on his feet. "I know," she said pitifully. "But it would feel that way now and later too."

He guffawed wildly. "You are very determined, my girl. And I love it. And I love delivering you this experience. Now get out and go help those strong men finish the job. The fun and the hotness are about to escalate as they handprint you all over with paint."

She had gotten so worked up in the moment that she had forgotten about the paint stipulation of the day's lineup of games. She grinned. She'd been excited about this part all day, but the heat of what she just enjoyed in the pool in the middle of the men had stagnated her brain.

"Yes, I'm very excited for that. And, you are right," she admitted as she watched the men getting back to work. "You always are, you know me so well."

"Yes, I do. Now get out and dry off so they can start laying their hands on you."

She hurried out of the pool at that thought and quickly swiped a towel across her flesh. She could see they were getting close to the painting stage, and that meant closer to her being fucked by them all.

Chapter 4

She snagged a quick snack, then rejoined the men. They were doing the finishing touches on the repairs, and Mason was stirring the paint. She hoped, with a chuckle, that John had purchased extra paint because she was so ready to be completely hand-painted by the men. Her lust was brimming over instantly as she saw Mason dip his hand into the paint with a huge grin.

Mason's gaze found her, and she held it with him. With a suggestive grin, he made his way towards her, white drips of paint falling off his hand like a hard rainfall.

She kept eye contact with him as he approached her.

"I guess being the paint stirrer, I get the first marking of you." Mason pressed his paint-coated hand to her torso, just below her right breast.

Laney instantly latched onto that idea and loved it. They were all going to be marking her as theirs with this hand-printing game. She was going to be theirs, all of theirs, for the evening, and that thrilled her. To be considered theirs for even a short time was a very delicious thought. Theirs to use, fuck, and pleasure as much as they wanted. It was a cornucopia of sex John was gifting them, and he'd get the champion belt because this would make Laney ravenous for him afterward and going forward. He was indeed supreme ruler and genius, which Laney never tired of awarding him.

"Brilliant. I love this," she squealed as she dipped her head down to observe the handprint he'd left on her flesh.

He grinned at her. "This is going to be fun."

Lance held up his hand in preparation for an announcement. "Remember, we can't just handprint her up. We have to actually paint, so this needs to be a slow progression." He laughed. "Otherwise, I'm so ready, I'd just take a roller filled with paint to her body myself and get to the game on."

The men all agreed with hollers and some clapping.

Laney's insides fluttered. She was going to be their main course. She loved that he wanted to quickly coat her body in paint to accelerate the show, and him talking to the men as if she weren't there settled nicely with her kinky self.

Her soul twirled in the sunshine and all the sexual energy emanating from their earnest faces. She couldn't be more ready for their orgy to start. She glanced at the house and saw John in the window. She wondered how much work he was really getting done. She honestly hoped he'd be watching once the sex started. That would be so hot. And if he interacted, telling the men what to do to her, that would launch her enjoyment of it to the moon.

They hurriedly organized their tools, ladders, and belts into a pile and began to grab paint supplies. First pouring paint into six trays, Lance divvied up the paint. He motioned them all over and soon everyone was ready to paint. John had taken the time to power wash it last weekend, telling Laney it was to wash the fence. She'd dumbly accepted that answer, not even considering this day would happen. She wasn't handy about such stuff, so she had taken it at face value. She loved that John plotted her sex dates far in advance. It made her intrigued, ever curious wondering what he was cooking up next for her. If they ever stopped the hotwifing, she didn't see herself ever falling back into their old mold of their marriage. It was forever new and exciting, and that alone made her want to stay with John for the rest of her life. He cared about her pleasure and gratification. To be prioritized so heavily and at the forefront of their relationship had made Laney want John more. It was having the opposite effect of what she'd have previously thought it would.

Marvin had been right. She needed more of Marvin and his wisdom, and so did John. But she also wanted more of Anderson. She'd found herself hoping lately that they'd become a throuple. Things were sort of there already since Anderson spent most nights at their house, and even had a section of the closet all to himself for clothes. It had been made more real when she'd started doing his laundry as well. She'd also been hoping he would appear today, being that he was near their ages, she'd had hoped he'd come join in the fun. He'd fit right in with this crew.

She bent over to pick up her tray. Just as she grasped the handle of the roller, she felt a wet hand pressed to her ass. "Oh," she said in delight with a wiggle of her body. "A hand on my ass. Whatever shall I do?" she asked playfully in mock shock. She danced after the hand left her body, showing off the handprint proof of her handled butt. "More please."

Another hand landed on her other ass cheek, and with a squeeze this time. Then one came as a single spank, which launched her body forward and she fell face-first into the grass.

"Oops," Jelson said before bursting into laughter. "That was a bit too hard."

She hadn't braced herself for a slap and the dude was strong as fuck. She felt her cheeks blush but secretly she loved a bit of humiliation, which was a kink she was still getting used to the reality of. She mused her sexuality was ever-evolving, and it was only happening because of her newfound openness.

She righted her body and raised her head, a filthy grin taking over. "And it's game on." She scoffed. "Again."

Jelson was clearly only too happy to repeat it as he smacked her bottom again, his hand full of fresh paint making a wet sound as it made contact.

She fell forward into the grass once more as they laughed at her again, and damnit if her clit didn't do a lurch. Her brain mulled over what the turn-on was for her with this. It was a new occurrence and though she could ruminate on it, the presence of it shocked her.

With a reddened face, she stood up and faced them. She smiled and shook her head, laughing also at herself.

The men all scattered with their paint and rollers. She carried her paint tray to the section of fence that Lance had assigned to her. She dipped the roller in it and buffed it along the ripples of the tray to squeegee off the excess paint. Slathering the paint across the partially stripped wood was satisfying with each roll. She felt accomplished as she quickly made progress covering the wood with the paint.

As she reached up high, an arm wrapped around her torso, and whoever it was planted a palm print below her left breast. She startled with jubilance and squeaked. "Oh, this is fun!" she exclaimed. She adored being touched, and having them guide it so each one was a surprise.

Alex whispered into her ear, "One more handprint closer to us getting to fuck you." It was just the kind of desirous threat she wanted to have whispered in her ear from a horny man behind her.

She nodded and glanced back at him, loving the fire in his eyes. "Yes, and please, keep going. I'm so ready!"

He pressed his other hand to her back. "Can't miss a spot John said."

She chuckled and squirmed. In truth, she was thankful for the painting task, it sort of distracted her while waiting for the big event. She was on edge, on the cusp of wanting to go and again beg John to allow it to happen now.

She rolled a few more runs with the roller before another hand smacked her ass. "Ow!" she yelled because that one hurt. She was thankful she had her footing so she didn't fall against the fence and get paint on her face.

Jelson heckled her from behind.

She was learning each of their styles, and Jelson was clearly a rough guy, which he'd admitted already, but which also turned her on. She'd learned she loved the full gamete of playful dominant aggression with men, and that she just loved them all in their own ways. She admittedly loved it when John got a little rough too, but she wasn't sure how she'd react going further into it. She couldn't wait to find out.

Skin smacks, grabs, finger presses, spanks, and slaps went on for the next twenty minutes. She glanced down at her almost fully painted body in amazement. This was the most unexpected day, and she couldn't be more thrilled.

"Wow, they are getting you pretty good here, aren't they babe?" John said, approaching while scanning her body.

"Yes, and I love the surprise of it all. I just love this, John! You are a genius!" she said in a high voice with excitement.

"I saw the spanks that knocked you over. How did that sit with you?" he asked as he lovingly caressed her face.

She felt her cheeks heat. "Well," she said with a significant pause. "I didn't expect to like it, but ..."

John shook his head as amusement filled his eyes. "But you did. I see perhaps a new kink birthing in you. We'll have to explore that, if you want."

She nodded but felt unsure. She wasn't entirely sure she openly wanted to acknowledge this, but she was filled with humility as she realized that hesitation was too late.

"So, they don't have to coat my face, right?" She wasn't too keen on the idea of having it all over her face, cum, sure, but not paint. Her skin felt tight with all the dried paint across her flesh.

He nodded. "Right. And I can't wait to see your body all painted when your suit gets removed. That's going to be hot. Like your sexy parts will be highlighted."

Lusty swirls of exhibitionistic excitement flooded her body as his words sunk in. "Oh, my. Hadn't thought of that. You really are brilliant!"

"Oh, babe, I'm just getting started." He ran his hand over her painted bottom. "This is pretty kinky, huh?"

"It is." She shimmied her body. "My skin is all tight feeling. It's oddly like a mild restraint, or the feeling of one."

"Well, we certainly are learning things today, aren't we?" His eyes were lit with lusty twinkling. "You okay with how rough Jelson is being, though? Be honest, babe, because I can shape that."

"Oh," she said releasing a big sigh. "That's actually been turning me on."

He raised an eyebrow. "Ah, okay. Interesting. Well, just wanted to check on you before things got really heavy here, or too far."

At the mention of that, butterflies of giddiness burst inside her. She was so excited to get fucked by all these young strong bodies that she felt slightly faint. She appreciated him watching over her, but she knew she had the power of her safe word to back her up.

"I'd better drink some water," she said, starting toward the house.

"Stay put. I'll get you a bottle of water."

John left and walked across the lawn. Lance was making his way towards John, and they met in the middle of the yard and talked briefly.

She loved that they were likely conspiring to create the best sexual experience for her. Damn, was she a lucky woman!

Chapter 5

Alex was making a beeline for her with two paint-coated hands. He grinned at her as he bent down and wrapped his hands around the tops of her feet. "Geez, you have tiny feet. I can almost smother the tops of your feet with just one grab."

She chuckled. "Yup, I'm size 6. John says I have the feet of a child."

He looked up at her. "Well, I'm enjoying this view. You're so damn sexy, Laney. I love your body." His eyes were filled with desire as he spoke.

"Thank you. I love hearing that." She filled further with cheer.

"And your personality is amazing. You're one amazing woman, Laney. I'm jealous of John being your husband," he said good-naturedly.

There was one thing that could make this day better, without a doubt. It was Anderson. She had been hoping that he'd still make an appearance before the group thing began. She had meant to ask John if he was coming too, but forgot with all the intensity of the goings on of the day. She'd loved when Anderson had unexpectedly appeared when she'd fucked Marvin. She was nervous about how strong her feelings for Anderson were growing and would that threaten her and John? She didn't think so, but the newness and the unforeseen occurrence of them were a little unsettling, to say the least. She cringed wondering how John would react, but she wanted to keep the lines of honesty open. John seemed to really like Anderson, but this was not just fucking anymore. This was eerily starting to feel like something else entirely. She never saw herself leaving John, no way, but she wasn't quite sure what to do with these blossoming feelings for Anderson. He wasn't just a cock on a killer body, he was an amazing man who continued to thrill, excite, and amaze her. And it felt dangerous, but it also felt incredible.

Her mind had wandered so much that she realized she'd mindlessly rolled the same section of fence several times. She dipped the roller in the waning puddle of paint in her tray as four hands landed across her body. She'd been so engulfed in her thoughts that she hadn't sensed their approach. Another pair of hands grasped her body. She looked at her section of fence and she had four more boards to coat in paint before her section was completed.

Lance appeared with a roller and began to cover those very planks. "Going to help you. We are all done, and you are almost fully covered in paint yourself."

She glanced down at her body; her front was mostly covered. She snickered. "Well, you'll all have to tell me if my backside is fully covered."

"Almost," Shane said as four more hands claimed her flesh with paint.

"Done," announced Mason. "You're a masterpiece."

"I'm really excited for you all to fuck me," she said with happiness. "And I'm still a bit shocked that I even get to say such a sentence. This has been a long-time fantasy of mine, just so you all know."

"Oh, we know. John has filled us all in on your likes, dislikes, wants, and desires. We know just what to do," Lance said with confidence and a giant smile. "And we can't wait to deliver."

His huge erection pressing out his pants confirmed this for Laney. She swiveled taking in all the sexy shirtless men and their bulky erections filling out their shorts. "I see your shorts have all gotten tighter."

They laughed along with her.

"Once you are dry, we'll begin," John said as he came upon the group. He had a very proud and happy grin and his eyes looked as excited as Laney felt. "Fence looks great. Thanks for all your hard work today."

"Our pleasure," Lance said. "Thanks for the job and the opportunity. And, most of all, thanks for Laney." He looked so happy and horny that Laney was about to fly up until she hit the clouds, she was so elated.

John caressed her painted body all over. "She feels dry." He scanned the men with an intense look in his eyes and ended his eye sweep by connecting with Laney's gaze. "Are you ready?"

She nodded, too excited to speak.

"They all know your safe word. I will be watching too, as will they. We will be also reading your facial expressions and your sounds. Obviously, I know those the best, so be totally open and don't mask your feelings so I can keep careful watch of this. I want you pleasured to the max and a cum soaked mess, so much so that you've never felt before."

She nodded.

"Give me words, Laney, not just a nod," John said sternly. "This is important."

"I understand. I agree. And I'm ready to be fucked to within an inch of my life by them." Her smile beamed brighter than the sun. She connected her gaze to each man. "Use me, fuck me, make me cum, on repeat, until I'm a floppy cum-soaked used whore, and ready for John like never before."

She held her head high, owning her own sluttiness, which she didn't consider sluttiness at all, but instead a higher-level sex goddess status. She would have likely been glorified in the way back generations of ancient times as a sex queen, a mogul of sexuality to admire, a blessedly gifted icon of femininity that most women would never even remotely be able to aspire to or boast about, but she claimed it. She owned it, and now she celebrated it with the help of her enlightened husband John. She felt the ancient spirits of similar women to her sexual caliber applauding her, dancing around her body in spirit form to prepare her for this impending sexual bliss, coming to her from a time long before all this current malarkey of controlling and diminishing women's sexuality had taken hold of today's cultures. A time when sexuality was seen as topmost in importance and not hidden, shamed, or denied of women, but instead glorified as the utmost importance in human existence. A time she'd have loved to have lived in. That was a whole different world she'd read about where openness in sexuality was revered and not boxed with the label of freak, but instead worshipped with admiration and awe.

John pulled her from her reverie as he grabbed her chin. "It's time." He raised his hands ceremoniously. "Men, I present to you my sexy wife, who desires very much that you fuck her, pleasure her, enjoy her as much as she will enjoy you all. Please, fuck my wife." He ceremoniously stripped her bikini top off and cut her bikini bottoms off her body with two swipes of his pocketknife.

She gasped as he plucked the fabric from between her labia lips and her ass cheeks and flung it to the wayside.

"I'll buy you a new one," he said with impish eyes.

The men filled her with more shameless passion as they oohed and ahhed, complimenting her body. She rolled in the midst of their attention, her arousal peaking the highest of the day so far.

John snapped a few photos of her front as she moved in different provocative poses, the other men did the same. John swirled his fingers and she swiveled so they could take photos of her backside. She bent over and spread her ass cheeks apart with her hands, and they groaned.

"Well, fuck," Alex said in a voice laden with want.

"Can't fucking wait to ride your body," Jelson said in a licentious voice.

The very air was seething with hypersexual energy as they all approached her. Inklings of electric fear and excited jitters sparked across her insides as they began to lay their hands on her. Lance pulled her body to his and while scooping the back of her head, he shoved his tongue into her mouth. His moan at their mouths colliding was delicious and it sent her sensuality into waves of passion as he pressed his hard cock to her belly.

Another man pressed his pelvis to her ass and began to thrust himself into the crevice of her cheeks.

Alex on her left caressed her left breast, and Mason on her right caressed her right breast.

"I'll take the less white meat," joked Jelson from behind.

It was funny, but she was too turned on to laugh. She wished she could see his dark flesh against her white-painted flesh. She imagined it must look beautiful to see an even greater contrast than just her natural flesh alone. The paint did alter the feel of their fingers on her, but it was no less erotic, just different, which in itself made it more erotic. Her brain latched on to the uniqueness of these sensations, and it increased her desire.

She undulated against all their touches, feeling floaty, as if they were keeping her upright, supporting her body against gravity by their fondling of her curves.

Lance tickled his fingers along her pussy lips, then spread them to press at and rub her slit.

"Very wet," he said with deep appreciation. "I love it."

She moaned, already feeling so deliciously overwhelmed by their claiming her body with theirs on all sides of her.

Lance pressed between the cleft of her mound and rubbed her clit.

She let him know he'd hit the right spot with her illicit moans as he expertly molested her fattening bean.

"Fuck, this is so fucking hot," Shane said with extreme relish.

"Been waiting to fuck you so hard," Lance said into her mouth.

"She's a fucking work of art," Mason said in a wanton jeer.

"No shit," said Alex. "Totally she is."

"Please, yes, please do," she pleaded, already feeling like a pile of loose flesh as her body's hormones exploded as he spanked her clitoris. "Oh, fuck, yessss," she slurred as she rolled her torso in response to his slaps.

Hands mauled her painted skin. Their caresses and grabs and her movement seemed to lessen the constricted feeling the dried paint had given her. She smiled as she imagined their firm strong grasps were making cracks in the paint.

She opened her eyes and spied John holding his phone up. Likely he was videoing it and she couldn't wait to watch it. She was so happy he was taking video and hadn't even realized she should have asked him to. But of course, John being John, he was filming it. This ramped up the salacious exhibitionistic experience for her. She glanced sideways across the yard. It was hot to her that it was a fact that her peeping tom neighbor could likely see this whole orgy launching from his living room windows.

"Laney, I told him about this, so he's watching," John said with lush carnality. "He just texted me."

"Oh, my Gawd, you did? He did?" She moaned in response. This knowledge of him watching torqued her enjoyment even higher. "Oh, that's so hot, John. Thank you," she cooed. They'd been a little reluctant at first to their neighbor's spying, but it had quickly grown into their mutual kink.

All the men's hands on her rolled her into a state of elation that burgeoned on weakness. She was at their mercy being outnumbered, but with John just mere feet away, she also felt very, very safe. This was a sexual haven like no other experience she'd yet encountered in her life.

Her moans and sighs filled the air as the men worked her body over. Their groans, grunts, and deep man growls filled her ever-growing desire.

"Fuck me," she said in a desperate depraved way, in as loud of a voice as she could muster, which wasn't much at all.

"With extreme pleasure, whore," Jelson said from behind as he bent her over.

She gasped in surprise.

Her face smacked into Lance's chest, and he quickly snatched her head between his large palms. He pressed his cock at her lips and she nodded. She opened her mouth, and he inserted his fat cockhead into her mouth.

She felt weaker yet, with pleasure filling her as Jelson stimulated her clit from behind, his rod pressed to her left ass cheek, wedged between their bodies.

The other men were still touching her nipples and tummy. They were caressing her erect nipples, squeezing her areolas. One of them snuck beneath her and began to suckle her nipples.

When Jelson pressed his cock to her wet hole, she groaned. She wanted to say, 'Yes please', but her mouth was full of Lance's cock. She squeezed his thighs in a death grip as Jelson penetrated her pussy.

He began to pump his meat into her slowly at first, but he ramped it up so quickly that it took her breath away. She found it hard to stay on Lance's cock like she wanted to with how forcefully Jelson was rocking her body from behind.

"Oh, shit yeah," Jelson slurred. "Take my fat big black cock, you slut." He smacked her ass as he fucked her, and she squealed a muffled shriek around Lance's cock inside her mouth.

Lance began to gently fuck her mouth and she prayed all the men would help hold her up because she was about to crumple to the ground with all this stimulation.

With her body like a wet noodle, she allowed her movements to flow with their manipulations of all parts of her. Someone on her left was thrusting his cock against her side, one was below her playing with her left nipple while deepthroating her right. The man on her right began to thrust his cock against her other side. She was being cock thrusted on four sides of her while the fifth man continued to stimulate her nipples from beneath.

She was surrounded, boxed in by cocks. It was cock heaven. The only thing better would be a titty fuck added in for the fifth cock, but that didn't seem physically possible. She was lulled back and forth, rocked between them as they enjoyed her body. They might be loving up thrusting their dicks on and in her, but none of them was being gifted the extreme level of heightened ripened pleasure she was enjoying. She loved the over-the-top stimulation from all of them across all parts of her body, and the mystery of not knowing on five levels of what she was to be given next.

Jelson began to hammer her backside, making her butt cheeks jiggle while his groans kept escalating. Whoever was beneath her began to pet her clit while still pinching a nipple and her rise to climax was near its end.

"Yes, get that clit, Shane," John instructed. "She likes a strong touch, so don't hold back."

Her body started to crumple as she neared the peak of her climax. It was so perfect to have Jelson jackhammering her G-spot while having her clit aggressively manhandled. She shuddered as the orgasm took a grip of her, and she started to fall off Lance's cock. He struggled but managed to keep himself in her mouth as he physically supported her body curl.

She released a muffled cry as she allowed the orgasm to take control. Her contractions erupted and rang out so intensely strong that she cried loudly and desperately wanted to smack the hand on her clit off.

Jelson pumped harder and then pulled his cock out, his hot cum spewing onto her back. "Paint you with my cum now," he muttered in a strained voice that was also filled with relief. "Aw, fuck that was a big load."

It felt like a big wet sploosh to Laney, too.

Jelson stepped back away from her and the man on her right quickly took his place and began to fuck her within seconds. Lance pulled his cock out of her mouth and they all rotated so that a new cock, Alex's thick dick, was now inside her orifice.

She wished Lance had come in her mouth, but she knew she'd get his cum soon, anyway.

Alex fucked her mouth a bit rougher, but it didn't turn her off, though she slightly gagged as he fucked.

He snickered. "Take my cock in your mouth, bitch."

John had done a good job telling the men she liked dirty talk and a bit of degradation because they were deftly meeting her wants for it.

Cocks were rubbing her body in multiple places, hands were constantly grabbing her, caressing her, squeezing her flesh. She was so turned on she wanted to scream and burst into a billion pieces across the sky and grass, she felt everywhere at once, yet inside herself as she moaned and rode the waves of orgasmic pleasure that were ever flourishing.

A rise to orgasm gripped her unexpectedly and she came hard again, her body twitching. The sensitive area of her clit was so strong she whimpered and all at once she wanted them right where they were and she wanted to hit them away. The big orgasm was even bigger than the last one and she felt herself start to fall. The men grabbed her on all sides and held her up as they continued to take their pleasure from her body as well as give it to her.

Whoever was in her pussy burst into a wild ramming spree, the skin smacks of him pounding his fat erection into her filled her ears.

"Fuck yes," Alex said as his body jerked against her head and his cum flooded her mouth.

She gagged but managed to swallow, most of it coming out the sides of her mouth. It was too hard to close her mouth fully around his cock as her vaginal walls contracted.

It was primal and wild, and she wafted into a floaty feeling as the hormones continued to flutter across her insides. She felt she could fly, soar through the air on these feelings alone.

"Keep it up, keep the pace strong, she'll keep coming harder and harder," John instructed.

Laney couldn't see him but hearing him really kept her feeling in the safe zone.

He pulled out of her cunt and his cum joined Jelson's on her back. Swiftly the men rotated again and she had new cocks in her pussy and her mouth.

They kept their attention on her clit, and she raged into a triple-peaked orgasm. She twitched and sputtered, barely able to keep up with all the sensations. Her body carried her careening into a frenzy of quick orgasms similar to what she'd experienced with her clit sucker when alone. Only then she had the power to pull the toy off when it got too intense, but now she was locked into enduring the intensity. She whimpered through the scrumptious agony of the multitude of orgasms that reined her whole body. She was helpless, she was their bitch, a floppy waif of a body as she fell into a state of reacting where she was essentially fully in her body just living through all she was feeling. This was real and she was legit in freeuse mode as they took their climaxes from her, sending streams of cum across her flesh on repeat. Being young men, they stayed hard and were able to come more than once. She couldn't count or keep track, but she'd felt way more than five splats of cum gracing her painted skin, that much she did know.

They continued to fuck, suck, caress, slap, and manhandle her as she slipped weaker and weaker, her strength usurped by orgasming so many times. She was drunk on her own orgasmic-induced hormones, as if she'd taken drugs. She craved collapsing to the ground and gave in. She began to fall, and they lowered her to the grass.

"Fuck her on the grass," John commanded.

The grass tickled her face as the men took up new spots against her ass, face, and sides.

"Let's flip her on her back," Lance said. "I think she needs a rest."

"Yeah," Jelson said in a soft compassionate voice.

They all gripped her body and limbs and flipped her over as if she were a quarter.

She sighed and giggled, the temporary reprieve from sexual stimulation helping her come down to reality a bit. "Wow, that was incredible. I feel so exhilarated, and like I'm in a dream."

The blaring sun made her squint when she looked at John on her left, so she turned her head straight to escape the brightness. Shane was preparing to enter her womanhood. He bent her legs back and lined up his cock before he roughly plunged in.

Her shoulders rose up at his dive in, then settled back to the somewhat prickly blades of grass as he began to pump himself into her. Mason kissed her, pulling her into a deep French kiss, her hand grinding into his scalp. The other men were on her nipples, and another pulled her hair into a ponytail and yanked it, then gently fingered it. She lamented that Jelson had forgotten that move when he'd taken her from behind, but was grateful to get it now.

Mason quickly jackhammered then creampied her with a yummy man grunt.

Jelson slipped in and fucked her cunt hole into another orgasm. He had the angle down just right and it had hit her clit perfectly making her come as if it were a real button.

Lance rolled her to her side and took her pussy again in what John always called a scissor position, which allowed him to give lots of firm attention to her clit. She came quickly, then again, the climaxes coming like rapid fire.

She grunted and groaned and felt more like a bird than a human as she relished the lofty feeling they'd fucked her into.

They started to slow down their touching of her as she kept her eyes closed.

"Yeah, I think she's about done," John said in a loving voice. "You've all fucked her into a coma," he said jokingly.

All Laney could do was smile as the warm sun caressed her body, the memories of them touching her still lingering across her flesh. She did want to fall asleep and felt she actually could.

"Anyone wants to snuggle her, go for it," John said in a tender voice. "I'll fuck her soon, but she could use a catnap with a warm body if anyone is willing."

She smiled at him giving her permission to sleep and as bodies cradled her on all sides, she allowed sleep to take her.

Chapter 6

She woke with a slow realization that she was naked and spread eagle in the grass. She recalled the men against her flesh, but now she was alone, though she could hear their voices laughing and talking. She smiled. They were having a good time, like a post fucking party. She was missing out, but she also knew she wanted the final act to happen before she moved. She wanted John to reclaim her and fuck her into several orgasms. She felt exhilarated, it was such a luxury to fall asleep after orgasming and John often gifted her that aftercare.

She raised herself up on her elbows, admiring the thorough hand-painting job they'd done on her. She imagined the dried cum on her back had been scraped off as she'd been fucked against the patch of grass beneath her, but some likely stayed adhered and she liked that knowledge. Her skin was saturated with paint and cum.

John approached her and knelt down. "Hi, babe, how do you feel?"

"Mmmm, I feel incredible." She beamed a big smile up at him.

"Two choices, do you want to shower and try to get this paint off before I fuck you, or do you want me to fuck you here, now, and in front of the men?"

"Here, now," she said with zero hesitation.

John smiled a thrilled smile. "Good girl," he said.

She knew he'd have said 'good girl' whichever she picked and that made her feel so safe and loved.

"You are the best husband in the world, my love," she cooed, squirming under his lusty-filled gaze down at her.

"I believe the best in the world applies to you."

He looked so hungry for her that it plumped up her desire for him instantly. "Daddy, fuck me, please, now. In front of the men."

He gave her a lascivious look that made her clit lurch, his desire to dominate her almost tangible in the air between them. "With great pleasure. You're mine."

"Mmmmm, good," she whispered softly, which didn't match her passionate desire for him at all. She was raging inside, but she still felt out of energy, despite the refreshing nap.

"Can you handle doggy? I want to fuck you doggy," John said in a firm attention commanding voice.

She nodded and rolled over, wobbling as she got on her hands and knees.

"Men," John called across the yard. "Can you be of assistance?" John asked urgently, and Laney instantly wondered what had him sounding that way.

They quickly joined them, obviously having jogged since they had arrived so swiftly.

"What's up, John? How can we help?" Lance asked in a pleasant eager tone.

"She can't do it. Each of you take an arm or a leg and hold her up so I can fuck my wife." He chuckled heartily. "This will be a different kind of group fuck."

Laney's excitement blossomed at this idea. She was going to be held securely on all sides by the men as they watched John fuck her. This was the most exciting part of the day.

She glanced back at John. "I love you, John. This is the raunchiest thing we've done, and I love you so much for it. Now fuck me hard as you can while these men brace me for your cock. Use me, your hole." Her being used kink was coming in strong as fuck with this one as the men all grabbed her limbs, and one man stood to brace her front, pressing his belly firmly to the top of her head. She realized it was Shane. She didn't need to use any muscles as they supported her, her belly dipping slightly. She figured she must resemble a fuck machine or heavy sex doll of sorts, and never in her life had she imagined this type of extremely taboo and devilishly naughty fuckery. It was ticking her kinky side to its most far-reaching boundaries, and she couldn't be more stoked to do it. John was going to use her well-used hole and these men were helping, she was in the golden zone of ecstasy. This was restraint play on a whole new level, one she'd likely never get graced with doing again.

John pressed his round cock head to her lips.

"Yessss, do it," she slurred, loving the firm pressing grips of all their hands holding her in place. "Fuck me with all their hands on me too."

"With total pleasure, my lovely wench of wife. Going to fuck your cunt like a beast until you come, then I fill you with my hot seed." His voice quivered with monumental want that warmed up her lust for him to savagely fuck her to the max heat level.

It was wretched, indecent, and she adored it. Anyone watching might surely get the wrong idea. That made it all the more perfect.

He began to ride her pussy, plunging his cock in by some monstrous code that ramped up faster and harder with each slam. He pressed his fingers into her hips and crammed himself in her to the tune of her accelerating moans.

She got a strange but arousing urge to wish the men would chant, make it seem even more like some kind of sex ritual of her man reclaiming her. She knew she'd better speak up or forever wonder if that would have added to the experience or not.

"Chant," she pleaded. "Chant 'fuck her, ram her, make her cum.'"

The men chuckled, but no one protested.

"Wow," said Lance. "Okay."

As John fucked her wet cum drenched sweet spot, the men chanted the phrase. One of them had hold of her clit and was circling and tapping it as John used her body for his own pleasure too.

It was like a dream unfolding as they began to slam her body into John's thrusts forcing her body to fuck John back.

She held her head firm against Shane's belly, watching his hard-on bounce below her face. She wished she'd had a longer tongue so she could have licked his dick.

She launched into the most ginormous climactic rise she'd ever experienced, her clit was screaming overly sensitive, throbbing, and aching as her body tried to crunch into a curl, but they held her so firmly she couldn't move. This was big, almost too much. She'd reached this top height with a sex toy once all by herself, where she'd gotten to focus on herself alone, but never this max with another human. It was massive, magnificent, glorious, but none of those words were enough to fit what she felt. It was majestic, and she was thrilled it was John who was inside her for it.

"Oh, fuck, shit, fuck," she spilled from her mouth as whimpering took over as the orgasm continued to intensify. She fell silent as she was royally overcome, her resolve completely undone. Her internal walls clamped down on John's erection repeatedly inside her and he released his usual groan as he came inside her, his body rocking into her bottom and thighs. He kept pumping himself into her, she assumed to let her milk him of every drop of cum and dribble that had been packed inside his balls from building all day long. Now what was once inside his body was now inside hers. And that was a sexy thought that she savored as he remained inside her.

They all stopped moving and just held her as John released his breath in excessive panting that seemed to go on longer than she'd expected it to.

She had been the tool and the vessel for all their pleasure, and it had been a spectacular honor. None of this would have happened without her, nor without John.

His softened cock slipped out of her, and he clutched at her body. The men shifted her to face him and then handed her off. She clung to him like a baby monkey, hugging him as close as possible, her chin resting on his shoulder. She wished she could ask them to take a picture of John holding like this because she wanted to see it, but it was too hard to speak. John was still panting pretty strongly, and her heart was still pounding. Her pussy was throbbing, and her entire body felt alive with pings of electricity. Her pussy felt a bit raw now, but she wouldn't have changed a second of what had just happened. Hell, she wouldn't have changed a single thing of the whole day. It was more perfect, more exciting, and more primally sexual than she'd ever gotten to be in her life.

"Thank you, baby. That was one of our best."

She nodded against his neck as she gripped him tight, squeezing her legs around him stronger. "Yes, it was." She sighed. "Maybe they could take a pic of us?"

John turned slightly before he called, "Anyone have a phone to take a pic? The lady wants a pic of me holding her like this."

She couldn't see John's face, but she could hear the happy smile in his tone.

"I do," Jelson said. "I got you guys. I'll take several from different angles." Jelson proceeded to take several pics, creeping around them, then coming up close for close-up pics. "Now, look at each other," he instructed. He sounded sweet and it added to the specialness of the moment.

Laney leaned back and looked into John's eyes. She saw love, satiation, joy, and bliss. She knew her own eyes must be mirroring those feelings back to John because she felt them too, her love for John had never been greater.

"Thank you," she said with emotions riding her hard enough for her need to suppress tears. "That was the most incredible crazy insane hot sexy wonderful experience of my life. All of it. And it's all because of you."

"It's because of you most of all, Laney," he said with emotional explosions going on in his eyes too.

Jelson kept taking pics as they kissed with a simple peck on the lips. "You two are damn priceless."

John nodded at Jelson. "Thank you, son, for taking those pics. And thank you all again for sending my wife into the most pleasure I think she's ever had." John gave her a questioning look.

"Yes, it really was. It was amazing, awesome, heroic! No words can justify."

The men smiled at her as John walked towards them still gripping her body to his. "A day for the books. You all executed that amazingly well, to the T."

Laney squirmed and John helped her to stand. She was a bit uneasy and swayed. He grabbed for her.

"You ready to walk yet? I can still carry you."

She laughed and stood her ground firmly. "I'm good. Just a bit like a bowl of Jell-O from all that sex and ecstasy." She beamed smiles at the young men and went to give them each a lingering hug and solid engaging eye lock. "Thank you," she said to each of them in turn. "You all are amazing and that won't be easily replicated, if ever." She released a big giant sigh. "Now, I'm ordering pizza because that turned me ravenously hungry. If I don't eat, I'm going to turn into a hangry bitch like you've never seen before." She laughed at herself. "Who's in for pizza?"

They all agreed, and she searched for her phone. "I have zero clue where my phone has gone."

"I've got it covered," John said, tapping into his phone.

She snatched her silky pale pink robe that John had so considerately hung over the patio chair and slipped it on. She'd seen them all sporting hard-ons again and she knew they'd be happy to fuck her for a round two. Which she'd love no doubt, but the events always ended with John fucking her, so that had to still be the plan for the end of the sex date. For now.

They all sat around the patio table with drinks and chatted while they waited for the pizza delivery.

"Any parts you hated?" John asked, which was one of his usual postcoital debriefing questions of her.

"Well, I don't love gagging," she said with a generous laugh.

The men chuckled.

"But it feels so good," Alex chimed in.

She remembered gagging on his cock. "Yeah, you should know!" she accused in a lighthearted tease.

"Oh, I can understand, but thanks for tolerating, because it does really feel amazing," Jelson said in an apologetic tone.

"Okay, no to gagging going forward," John said in a serious tone.

"Well, I didn't die, I guess," she said with a scoff and deep humility. "It's physiological, not personal. I get it."

"And funny," Shane said jokingly. "Just kidding. Well, not really. Sorry, not sorry. But, we did give you orgasms right back."

She rolled her eyes with a big smile. "I guess it's okay, I can tolerate it, but you'll need to please me right back hardcore to get me where I was before it, cause it definitely puts a halt on my enjoyment."

"Noted," John said, though he'd never really pushed her that far like these men had today.

She attributed their liking of it to the larger watching of internet porn these men had likely grown up watching, cause that was a thing.

"So, we did okay, Laney? Not too far for you?" Lance asked with genuine concern.

"No, if you had, I'd have said my safe word." She touched his arm and made eye contact. "You all did amazing. Out of the park, honestly."

The pizzas arrived and they enjoyed an evening of drinks and hot yummy pizza. When the young men left, John pulled her into a hug and touched his forehead to hers. "Seriously, be honest. What are your thoughts on how it went down, now that it's over? This is the most extreme thing we've done so I need to know."

"Incredible. I loved it." She smiled back at him, allowing all her love for him to show in her eyes. "They picked me up and I was like a puppet, your own living pocket pussy." She laughed animatedly. "It was hot!" she exclaimed with laughter still ringing in her words.

He joined in her laughter. Once it calmed down, with mirth sparkling in his eyes, he asked in a more serious voice, "But, in true disclosure, anything you'd change if we ever did this again?"

She nodded, debating if she should say it. "Anderson. I'd love to have Anderson here too." She watched his face for any negative reaction but saw none.

"Yeah, I told him about this but he had a big job today and he'd said he'd make it if he could. I would have liked him here as well."

She relaxed, quite happy John was feeling a fondness for having Anderson around too. "He's coming here after work, right?"

"Yeah, he texted me an hour ago saying they are almost done."

"Good, it will be good to see him after all that. He's kind of becoming like a staple around here." She again watched his face closely.

He maintained a pleasant easygoing expression. "Agreed. I'm really enjoying him too, Laney. And I love how he is with you."

"Good. I know we may lose him to some pretty young thing someday, but I'm glad to have him while we get him." She felt stirrings of dread form in the pit of her stomach. That was a fear that had been corrupting her insides for a while, so it was healthy to say it out loud and acknowledge it.

"Yep, and honestly, as much as I want him to stay with us, we need to be fair. He's young and has his whole life ahead of him."

She nodded. "Yes agreed." She didn't want that day to come, but regardless, she had this new version of John, and all the orgasms she could endure. "I can't tell you how many times I came today but it was way in the double digits. Likely thirty or forty." She tipped her head to the side. "More likely forty."

He corralled her body to his, grabbed her hand, and led them forward to the sliding glass door. "Now, let's go get you a shower, my sexy paint queen."

She giggled and entered the house, the blast of air conditioning hardening her nipples against the silky fabric.

John glanced down. "Well, hello, that's a turn-on. But I'm letting your pussy rest. That was a lot of cock."

She released a bolt of laughter. "You're telling me! But if you can catch me, you can fuck me again." She squealed as he lunged for her, missing on purpose.

She bounded up the stairs with John close on her heels.

The End, for now...
Get the next books in the series: Anderson Comes Home, And Servicing the Dryer Repairman, Laney Gives a Tip

About the Author

Ruan Willow is an erotica author, sex blogger at https://ruanwillowauthor.com/ , sexuality and erotica fiction podcaster at the Oh F*ck Yeah with Ruan Willow Podcast[1] , and an audiobook narrator/ voiceover actor. She is also published on Medium https://medium.com/@ruanwillow, Frolic Me, and Literotica, and coming soon on Theo Reads. She loves spending time with family and friends, interacting with fans, cooking, sharing/chatting with and educating people about sex, reading, travel, being outdoors, swimming, learning about sex, podcasting, and more sex. Did you catch all the sex? She's giggling right now thinking about you reading all about sex. She values openness and talking about the natural act of sex. And. Yup, she loves to laugh!

---

1. https://ohfckyeahwithruanwillow.buzzsprout.com/

Thank you!

Thank you to all my family and friends who support me. I wouldn't be where I am without you. You are all the magic and the light in my life, the love that grows in my love. I am honestly thrilled and humbled by the supportive people in my life. Love you!

To Fans:

Thank you for purchasing and/or reviewing this book!

I peddle fantasies for the purposes of your enjoyment, entertainment, and expanding your sexuality and openness. Always remember that no fantasies are bad. You should enjoy your sexuality and your fantasy life as much and as often as you can.

Thank you for reading my book! I write for myself and for my fans. My fans are my main focus though, but of course, I want to like what I write too, and I thoroughly enjoyed writing these stories.

In writing erotica/erotic romance, I'm always excited for the erotic journey! I'm on a path of sexual empowerment, enlightenment, and enjoyment. Thank you for reading this and I'm honored to be a part of your journey as well.

I am where I am because fans have responded to me and my content, so I owe everything to you! Thank you! Thank you! Thank you! You are a blessing in my life, and you give me more joy than you will ever know. I love interacting with all of you and I will never give that up.

My stories are erotica, so they have a generous amount of sex in them, as I believe our relationships should have as well. I hope you enjoyed this novella for what it is, literature that is in the erotica genre. It is very different from the romance genre, and there are different levels of heat in the erotica genre as well. Explore them all!

If you'd like more of my work, please see below for my list of published works on the following pages, visit my sexuality and erotica podcast, find my audiobooks, visit my website, my Patreon, visit my profile on Medium, and my linktree with all my links at https://linktr.ee/RuanWillow

Thank you for purchasing this book, I'd love to hear your thoughts in an honest review on the site where you purchased the book from. I'd absolutely love it if you shared my book with others. It warms my heart profusely when I see someone who has taken the time to review/share my book. Love you all very much!

All my best, yours truly, with overflowing love from a full heart,

Ruan Willow

Erotica author, sexuality/erotica podcaster, and erotic book narrator

Ruan's books and audiobooks: https://books.ruanwillowauthor.com/

All Ruan's links in one spot: Ruan's links[1]

---

1.   https://linktr.ee/RuanWillow

Oh F*ck Yeah with
Ruan Willow Podcast

It's free on podcast apps! Also airing on the internet radio station Full Swap Radio website and app Tuesdays and 6 pm CST, and Wednesdays 8 am (subject to change, check for the current schedule online) AND the PodNation TV Network/Roku TV station/Fire TV/powered by Podnation Pods anytime VOD on the app, and Sundays and Mondays After Dark Hours around 11 pm Eastern Time Zone (subject to change).

Oh F*ck Yeah with Ruan Willow Podcast on Buzzsprout[1]

---

1. https://ohfckyeahwithruanwillow.buzzsprout.com/

Ruan's other books and novellas:

All books: https://storyoriginapp.com/collections/81018450-74cc-4038-888f-f2c13e356054

https://books.ruanwillowauthor.com/

Ruan's Getaway Series: Heterosexual, MILF Age Gap

The Sex Challenge Series: Heterosexual, Middle Aged 2nd Chance I Dare You

The Stars Aligned Series: Heterosexual, Twenty-Something's

Skinny Dipping at the Pond on a Hot Summer Day, Book 1 (ebook & audiobook)

https://books.ruanwillowauthor.com/skinnydippingatthepondonahotsummerday

Spring Break *(college aged multiple partner fantasy books)*

Spring Break & Stranded with Her Best Friend's Brothers, Books 1, 2, and 3.

GET THE SPICIER VERSION by RuAnn Willhoe Spring Break & Stranded with Her Best Friend's Brothers Plus 6 Men, on Smashwords.

Next Door Temptations (*middle aged couple, second chance at love and sex, friends to lovers*)

Next Door Temptations, Book 1 (in ebook, audiobook) and book 2.

Seducing Her Ex's Best Friend (*a story of revenge, angst, deception, and romance, HEA*)

Seducing Her Ex's Best Friend, Book 1 (in ebook and audiobook)

Wingless Hunger (*HEA Romantasy, book 1*)

Standalone's:

Decadent Erotica, An Anthology: 10 Tales of Extreme Sensuality, Indulgence, Dominance, and Submission (in ebook, paperback &

audiobook

She Dominated Him Out of a Speeding Ticket (Female Domination story) (ebook and audiobook):

Never Say, Never Swing (a first-time swinging story) (in ebook & paperback coming in audiobook)

Magic In Her Kisses (woman loving woman Domme/sub BDSM) (in ebook, paperback, & audiobook)

The Mardi Gras Unmasking (reverse harem) (in ebook & paperback)

The Licking Sip Coffee Shop (a steamy explicit coffee shop)

Neighborhood Sex Secrets (in ebook and paperback)

Santa Gives the 12 Orgasms of Christmas

The Sugar Daddies (in ebook, paperback, and audiobook)

FRIENDS WITH BENEFITS: A Spicy Four Short Story Adventure (in ebook, paperback, and audiobook)

Spicy & Wicked Tales (in ebook and audiobook)

Hookups & More? (in ebook and audiobook)

Weekend Hotwife Surprise (in ebook, coming in audiobook)

SFW Fantasy audiobook novel narrated by Ruan:

Heroes of the Caroylngian Age written by author Joseph Samaniego:

Neighborhood Sex Secrets

<u>https://books.ruanwillowauthor.com/neighborhoodsexsecrets</u>

A very steamy sexually adventurous story of a woman embracing her entire sexuality and in doing so, claiming her empowerment.

Alexa has missed out for long enough. Life with her ex had stuck her with a vanilla sex life. All the deep, dark fantasies she had hidden away began to bubble up once she became single. Her journey toward sexual freedom skyrocketed when she learned about neighborhood sex secrets at a pool party where she was suddenly calling two neighbors 'Daddy'. As she melted into the secret sex world emerging before her in the seemingly boring square mile of homes, she deliciously found herself assimilating into the hidden underworld of an alternative lifestyle.

Her sexual explorations exploded as she let go of traditional societal conventions and chose to take chances. Instead of playing alone in her bedroom, she began to live out the raunchiest depths of her fantasies as her new partners set out to help her fulfill her sexual bucket list. Alexa spread her wings doing taboo acts in real life that, until then, she'd only watched on a screen or lived merely in her dreams. Her Daddies became her guardians, deliverers of her desires, and directors of sexual heights she never thought were possible.

But then her new world gets threatened. Someone doesn't want her in the new triad of Daddy, Daddy, and good girl. Not only can the good guys turn bad, but bad guys also come back, and only the protected good girls can withstand the storms. Through it all, she finally understands one thing for sure, she is most definitely a good girl, and good girls have the most fun when they follow their 'Daddies'.

An HEA Daddy Dom/submissive story of control and submission that flourishes as mutual sexual freedoms. The book contains elements of mild BDSM, multiple partners, exhibitionism, cheating, experimentation, and lots of pleasure. ALL acts are consensual and characters are 18 and over. Enjoy a story of fantasy later-in-life exploration into open sexuality.

Anthologies and Award Nominations

Ruan has stories in the following anthologies:
He Will Obey (which was AWARDED THE 2020 SILVER PIGTAIL IN BEST
ANTHOLOGY CATEGORY
The Femdom Coven (nominee for 2021 Golden Pigtail Smut Awards)
Inside of Ruan Willow (also available in an audiobook)
(this audiobook was a nominee for the 2021 Golden Pigtail Smut Awards)
Decadent Erotica An Anthology **3rd Place Winner in the 2022 Golden
Pigtails Smut Awards for Dark/Taboo Category**
Nominations for the 2023 Golden Pigtail Awards include:
Servicing the Trash Man, My Filthy Hotwife Adventure
Dressing Room Domme
Anthology Ruan has a story in titled Hearts and Flowers, Whips and Chains

Ruan is in the following Femdom anthologies:

He Will Obey (stories of female domination)
The Femdom Coven (erotic horror and fantasy)
Hearts and Flowers, Whips and Chains (stories of kinks & power
exchanges)

Other links:

https://books.ruanwillowauthor.com/
Ruan's website with free erotic stories Ruan Willow Author[1]
Ruan's Patreon Ruan Willow on Patreon[2]

Ruan Willow on Goodreads Ruan Willow Goodreads Author page[3]

Ruan Willow on BookBub https://www.bookbub.com/profile/ruan-willow

Sign up for Ruan's newsletter: https://subscribepage.io/ruanwillow

Subscribe to Ruan's Substack (Free and paid levels) https://ruanwillow.substack.com/

Ruan Willow on Medium: https://medium.com/@ruanwillow

ARC copies are usually on BookSirens and StoryOrigin App. Check those sites for FREE ARC of books and audiobooks.

---

1. https://ruanwillowauthor.com/

2. https://www.patreon.com/ruanwillow

3. https://www.goodreads.com/author/show/21312130.Ruan_Willow